BETTER LIVING THROUGH

Alchemy

Broken Eye Books is an independent press, here to bring you the odd, strange, and offbeat side of speculative fiction. Our stories tend to blend genres, highlighting the weird and blurring its boundaries with horror, sci-fi, and fantasy.

Support weird. Support indie.

brokeneyebooks.com
facebook.com/brokeneyebooks
instagram.com/brokeneyebooks

BETTER
LIVING
THROUGH
Alchemy

BETTER LIVING THROUGH ALCHEMY
by EVAN J. PETERSON

Published by
Broken Eye Books
www.brokeneyebooks.com

Cover illustration by Matthew Cunningham.
Cover design by Matthew Cunningham and Scott Gable.
Interior design and editing by Scott Gable.

Temple Laboratories artifact 13

978-1-940372-73-0 (trade paperback)
978-1-940372-74-7 (hardcover)

BETTER LIVING THROUGH Alchemy

For Kellie —
Take bardo.
Be god. 8/25/24

[signature]

Evan J. Petersen

DANCING AT THE END OF DAYS

Tuesday, December 31

VEN AS SHE DANCED, TRYING TO LOSE HERSELF IN THE PIT, TONYA COULDN'T ignore the feeling that her left arm had somehow returned. On stage, Electric Pentacle thrashed on their guitars and fondled their synthesizers, building the energy of the crowd as midnight crept close. The light-wave conductor played her oscillator, its white and red pulses building in frequency, ultimately mimicking the contractions of orgasm. On the threshold of the new decade, the fans pumped their limbs and swayed in the atomized sweat of the nightclub.

Tonya had never experienced a phantom pain—or phantom anything, really—since losing the arm in the crash years ago. Even in her dreams, she rarely noticed its presence or absence. She looked at the place where it would've been, imagining what it would look like to see both of her own brown hands swooping through the air, jiggling her tank top to get some air on her skin. She *could* feel it though, the air against it, its weight descending from her shoulder. For a moment, Tonya thought she could even feel sweat running down it.

Whatever was in this new shit, it was damn good.

The guy who sold it to her would only give her one, though she tried to buy more. "It's strong. Really strong. One is all you need." He looked like every other pale young guy in the music scene. He collected her cash and wished her a Happy New Year. She popped the bardo into her mouth and swallowed. It had the faint glue-like taste of any other gel tab.

Tonya didn't know what to make of a dealer who didn't want her money. She didn't meet a lot of guys in general who discouraged her from getting wasted. She'd never tried bardo before, but it was New Year's Eve.

The boy dancing behind her sidled up and put his hands on her hips. She glanced over her shoulder to make sure it was the same guy from before, the adorable one in the Silver Ash Cure tee. It was. Tonya leaned back into him, and he wrapped his wet arms around her waist. She could feel his cock against her, hard already in his jeans. *You better get hard when I put it on you,* Tonya thought.

The Pentacles continued their pulsing rhythm while the singer stopped to make an announcement. "All right, my psychonauts! We're thirty seconds from midnight. Are you ready?"

The crowd cheered as one organism, troubling the line between orgy and hivemind. A girl approached and embraced Tonya from the front. White skin, blonde hair, pink peasant blouse—a crunchy hippie vibe. Exactly Tonya's type. The girl took a drag from her vapor wand, and Tonya opened her mouth, tongue wagging and beckoning. The blonde closed her mouth over Tonya's, exhaling the cloud into her lungs as their tongues met.

"Ten! Nine! Eight!"

The crowd chanted along with the Pentacles.

"Seven! Six!"

Her skin glistening in the throbbing light, Tonya felt like she was about to break apart into a thousand hummingbirds, each with nectar running through its tiny veins. The drug was kicking in much faster than she'd expected.

"Five! Four!"

The boy pressed against her from behind. The girl pressed against her from the front. Tonya closed her eyes as the vapor high mixed with the bardo high, and there it was: the moment everyone was chasing, the moment when the entire ego crumbles to glitter and there is only pleasure, right down into the soul.

"Three! Two!"

She was everywhere and nowhere. She was everyone and everything, only a vague memory of being separate. It was peace and ecstasy in one, rapture and satori.

"One! Happy New Year!"

She opened her eyes, and just for a couple of seconds, she saw it—her left arm, whole and dark and perfect. Through the haze of it all, she didn't question it. It made sense. Most dreams make sense while you're in them.

That's the moment Tonya's joints came apart, the invisible seams of her body opening, and she fell in pieces to the floor. The boy behind her was left holding her disembodied head. They didn't even know each other's names. The look on his face was the last thing Tonya registered before her brain shut down.

Wednesday, January 1

As expected, Critter was already in the office when Kelly arrived at 10:35. The pins and needles in her left leg sparkled extra this morning, and she had to rely on her wooden cane. The city smelled strange today, stranger than usual. Under the rain and the traffic and the waters of the Puget Sound, something new fermented. Kelly wondered when it would bubble to the surface.

"Morning! You're later than usual today," Critter said without looking up from his laptop.

"I'm the boss. That's why I have an employee," Kelly clapped back. She picked up the mug of cold black coffee Critter had prepared for her a half hour earlier. She slurped the sour liquid and read the black graphic on the clover-green mug out loud. "'Keep Calm and Worship Cthulhu.' That's cute. What happened to my 'Seattle is Wet' mug?"

"Dropped it. Sorry." Critter sipped from his iced latte in the disposable cup. "Thought I should buy you a new one. Aren't you going to microwave that?"

"That's rich coming from you—the iced-coffee queen. Did I miss anything?"

Critter severed his gaze from the screen and looked at her. "Actually, quite a bit. We had a walk-in. On New Year's of all days. Rich by the look of her. I told her to come back at 11. Figured you had to be here by then. You better land this client. Also, have you seen the news?"

Kelly frowned and stared into her new mug. "You know I haven't. What fresh apocalypse is it now?"

"Hey. Look at me," Critter said. "Are you okay?"

She looked into his hazel eyes, gilded with forest green eyeliner. "Yes. I'm okay. Rough night. And my neuropathy is killing me today."

Critter furrowed his brow. "Please tell me you didn't drink alone."

Kelly gave the kind of pursed smile most people would give a panhandler.

"I swear I didn't. That's part of the problem. I was alone on New Year's Eve. It brought back some bad memories."

Critter got up from his desk and gave her a hug. "I'm sorry, Kel. You could've come out with me and my crew."

She slumped. "That might be even worse. The tagalong older chick out with the boys, trying to have a good time."

Pulling back from the hug, he cooed. "Oh, come on. You're thirty-two. What happened to that whole, 'Old enough to know better, young enough not to give a rat's ass,' thing you were doing?" Then with a distinctly different tone, "Tell me again why we're working today?"

"We're getting caught up. And this isn't a real holiday, Critter." Kelly poured the rest of her coffee into a potted plant on top of the microwave.

"Hey!" Critter said. "What'd you do that for?"

"I'll make fresh!" she said, grabbing a coffee pod.

"No, dingus! You just killed my bromeliad!" Critter walked over and grabbed a handful of paper towels, attempting to soak up the excess coffee.

Kelly gritted her teeth. "I thought coffee grounds were good for them?"

"Should I come back again in another hour? Or not at all?" A woman lingered in the hallway. Kelly didn't like the smell of her. A little too much sandalwood and way too much entitlement.

She was tall, about six foot to Kelly's five seven and dressed in an expensive-looking camel peacoat. Her inky black hair and olive skin shone with what little gray sunlight came in through the office windows. "Sophia Martinetti," she said, strolling in without offering her hand to shake.

Kelly shot a look at Critter who clutched the flowerpot and returned with it to his desk. "Kelly Mun. Welcome to Non-Linear Investigations. Or . . . welcome back."

Sitting in Kelly's office behind a closed door, Martinetti got down to business. Almost. "Did you know that *nonlinear* isn't hyphenated? Do any of your clients bring that up?"

Kelly played cool. A rich client was a rich client, and most of them tested her the way they would test a carnival palm reader. "I learned that after I got my business license. It works though. Easier for the clients to sound out. Not everyone who hires me is a native speaker."

Martinetti smiled almost as though flirting. "Neither is every private investigator. But you are. Korean dad, white American mom, born right here in Seattle."

Kelly stayed even. "Very good. You've done your research."

Martinetti gave a subtle shrug and looked around at the little office. "I like to know what I'm buying."

This lady was pushing it. The roadside finds and assemble-it-yourself furniture in Kelly's office embarrassed her, but she would not tolerate a client looking down on her. She gave a little attitude back.

"Miss Martinetti—I assume it's *miss* since I don't see a ring—if you're this good at finding out about people, why do you need me?"

Martinetti leaned in. There was something predatory in her body language, like a viper coiling up to strike. "I thought that would be obvious. My people are awfully literal. I need someone more oblique. Esoteric. That's what you do, right?"

Kelly nodded. The woman wasn't just rich enough to look great; she was also compulsively fastidious. Her skin was flawless. Her hair was perfect. Her eyebrows were perfect. *She* was perfect. Kelly felt an uneasy mix of attraction and resentment.

Martinetti continued. "I don't like getting my hands dirty. You do. And you're very good at it from what I've seen."

Martinetti smelled like blood now. Blood and money—how cliché. Without meaning to, Kelly broke her composure for a moment and grimaced.

"And how much of my work have you seen?"

Martinetti continued to smirk flirtatiously. "Enough to earn me as a client. You should charge more."

Kelly laughed and tapped an unpainted fingernail against her desk. "You can tip if you like."

Sophia Martinetti finally stopped pussyfooting around her real interest. "And though I can't be sure, I'd wager that you're psychic. You cloak it well, but you're a little too good. Maybe not advanced enough for national or corporate security, but you're no showbiz charlatan. My guess is . . . psychometry?"

"Ha!" Kelly said. "I wish I was a toucher. Nope. Clairolfaction."

Martinetti's eyes lit up as she sounded out the sensuality of the word. "Clair-ol-faction!" She moistened her dark-red lips with her pale tongue. "That's a rare one. You should've gone into luxury brands. I know a perfumer in New York who could use a woman like you. May I pass your name along?"

"Do whatever you want. So now that you know I can smell bullshit, you can drop this executive dominatrix act. Talk to me, one professional to another. What can I do for you?"

Sophia Martinetti raised an eyebrow. She straightened her posture but didn't act quite as haughty. "Miss Mun, are you familiar with something called bardo?"

"Hmm. *Bardo* is a Buddhist term. The in-between place. The mists between one life and the next incarnation."

"Correct, and it's also the street name for a new recreational drug. Extremely new."

Kelly turned to her computer and typed in search terms: "bardo" and "drug." No leads.

"Not a lot out there on it."

Sophia stood and walked to the single window. "There won't be. It's only been on the street for about a month as far as I can tell. The cops haven't even picked up on it yet. But my people have. It looks like someone's testing it here in Seattle—figuring out the market, getting people interested. Maybe other places too, but I haven't been able to find anything beyond the city. Nothing in Portland or San Francisco or the usual smuggling ports. Nothing beyond the continent."

Kelly stared at Sophia. The woman certainly enjoyed playing up the drama. "Is it habit-forming? Any fentanyl connection?"

"We don't know that yet either."

Kelly took a deep breath. The conversation smelled like damp caves and decaying wood and hidden things. It smelled like a mystery but not a lie. "The name makes me assume it has something to do with disassociation. Is it like ketamine? Or Ambien with a psychedelic kick?"

"Could be. Someone overdosed on it last night at the Deep."

Kelly's stomach sank. She prided herself on staying on top of the news. Anything could be a lead in her business, and the strangest things often were.

"Ugh. I should've known that before you got here . . ." The two women went quiet while Kelly typed and scrolled. "Huh. The death at the Deep has no drug connection in the news. And that doesn't sound like any kind of OD I've ever heard of. What makes you think that this woman was on bardo when she died?"

Martinetti stared out the window. "I have my ways."

"I'm sure. So what do you need me to find out?"

"At this point?" The client turned and walked back to her seat. "Everything. Assume I don't know anything about bardo. I haven't been able to get a hold of it or figure out who's manufacturing it. I need you to find out everything you can. What's in it, what it does, who makes it, who's selling, who's buying."

Martinetti's phone buzzed in her pocket, and she checked it and rolled her eyes. She tucked it back into her pocket.

Kelly asked, "And what about your other agents? The 'awfully literal' ones as you call them?"

Martinetti smiled. "I'm sure they won't get in your way. Or vice versa."

Kelly smelled the ozone scent of omission now. Not the acidic scent of a lie but getting there. Something was cloaked, either with magic or some other subterfuge.

"How much danger will I be in?"

Martinetti leaned into her chair, falling back into that initial flirty tone and body language. "That depends how deeply you go. The deeper into the abyss, the more likely you'll find monsters."

Kelly smiled and relaxed a bit herself. "Is that a pun? On the Deep?"

Martinetti rolled her eyes again. "I wish. You know how these things work better than I do. Glaring coincidences that lead nowhere. Tangents that seem barely connected but prove to make all the difference. But I'm not joking. Literally or metaphorically, I expect you're going to find some monstrous things."

Kelly stared Martinetti in the eye for an uncomfortable moment. Like an abyss herself, Martinetti stared right back.

Kelly grew impatient and broke the silence. "I happen to know someone who's quite fond of monsters. And the monsters are quite fond of him."

Martinetti smiled back. "Yes, your lobby boy. He's a darling one, isn't he? Have you ever made a pass at him?" She looked past Kelly at the pressboard bookcase behind her. Another sidetrack, most likely intentional to test Kelly's focus.

"If you really did your homework, you'd know he's my cousin. Mom's side obviously. I love him." She watched as Martinetti's eyes darted around slightly, probably reading the book titles on the shelves behind Kelly or coming up with her next quip. "But I don't want to fuck him. Or you, Sophia."

The businesswoman's attention locked back onto Kelly, reassessing her. Then she said, "That's too bad. You're very pretty. But back to the point. I doubt either of you will want to arm wrestle with these monsters. I will, of course, compensate you accordingly."

"I won't break anyone's kneecaps, Sophia. And I don't deal with mafia."

"I won't ask you to, Kelly. And I'm not mafia. I'm a businesswoman."

"You realize that is exactly what someone in the mafia would say, right?"

The mysterious client sighed with impatience. "I need a detective, not a thug. I need to know the true impact of bardo on my business."

"Which is?"

Martinetti's face went soft and blank. "Research and investment."

Kelly shrugged. "The more I know, the better I can help you. What do you think bardo is?"

"It's magic, of course. A literal magic pill. You saw what happened to that girl in the photos. I suspect it's a product of alchemy, but my other investigators have come up short. Even the psychics—but I suspect they're too cozy in their assumptions. They're missing something that I want you to catch."

Kelly started to fidget. "I don't know if I wanna step in a shit pile as deep as this one."

"You can drop the assignment at any point, provided you communicate everything you find out. And no need for heroics. I need you to stay crisp and alive to report back to me. Go deep, come back in one piece, and for gods' sake, do not sample the bardo if you find some."

It was a tempting offer. Martinetti would know business was slow. She was good enough at this game that she didn't even need to taunt Kelly about it.

"I'm still not totally convinced, Sophia—and that's not hardball. It's self-preservation. What happens if and when I find out too much? Will you and your people try to wipe me out? I told you I don't do mafia assignments."

Martinetti took a moment to stare at Kelly and then look around her meager office again. "We'll wipe out your debts maybe. Paying people off is much easier than making them disappear, I find. If you learn too much, my first recourse is to reward you for good, effective services and offer to hire you full time. Just don't go catching a guilty conscience. I hear those are highly contagious, especially if you don't wash your hands."

Kelly almost sneered but swallowed her pride. "You drive a hard bargain, Miss Martinetti. Fuck it. I'll take it. That'll be a thousand as retainer to start. I bill sixty an hour. I'll let you know when we're getting close to fulfilling the first thousand. You can pay Critter—Christopher—on the way out. For your privacy, we have a cloaked account."

Martinetti laughed and got up to leave. Kelly couldn't tell whether it was the laughter of mockery or genuine appreciation. With her back to Kelly, the businesswoman said, "I'm sure you've cloaked a lot of things. Your lease here for one. I expect you're not paying what this space is worth. I applaud that. You're a natural witch, whether you know it or not."

Kelly got up to show her out, and Martinetti half-turned and gave some side-eye. "You're discreet, and you know enough hoodoo to be slippery. I need a woman like you working for me right now. Look further into what happened at the Deep last night. Then you'll start to grasp what we're dealing with."

When she'd gone, Critter whistled. "You really charmed her, didn't you? She paid triple the retainer and told me to bill double the hourly rate you quoted."

Kelly didn't speak. It was easy to smell a devil's bargain, but she still couldn't detect which circle of hell the sulfur came from.

"Jee-zus fuck. What am I looking at here?" Critter scrolled through an image search as Kelly watched over his shoulder. Pics of the dead woman leaked immediately, long before the police got to the club. Her body had been divided into six pieces—head, torso, and four limbs—like some perverse hexagram from a desecrated *I Ching*.

"Gimme a sec." Critter opened some links to various social accounts. They didn't even need to go deep or check the hexweb. Kelly didn't hold off.

"It looks like someone cut her to bits in front of hundreds of people at the Electric Pentacle show. But our client is sure this was a drug overdose."

Critter leaned in, squinting at the details of a photo, and then he leaned back and used zoom. "Comments are saying that she fell apart. Just fell apart . . . hmm . . . her name was Tonya Williams . . . from Portland . . . she followed the Electric Pentacle here on their tour. There's a good lead. Know anything about Electric Pentacle or Silver Ash Cure? That was their opening act."

Kelly sniffed for anything she could detect. Digital data rarely yielded much psychic information. "Well, they're bands, obvi. Synth metal, I think. Not my thing. Which band was on when she . . . disintegrated?"

Critter scrolled. "Looks like Electric Pentacle. That's a Hodgson reference. Hodgson's Carnacki stories had an electric pentacle—a protection charm that Carnacki would make out of electric lights arranged into a traditional pentagram sign. Pretty good at keeping out malevolent spirits. Not foolproof though."

"Hodgson was, what, Victorian era?"

"Just missed it. Edwardian. British, pre-World War I. The Carnacki stories anyway."

"Hmm . . . anything else stick out about the music?"

Critter typed and scrolled. "'Silver Ash Cure' is a reference to H.H. Holmes, the World's Fair serial killer. Gross. Both bands are on the Redchapel record label."

Kelly sniffed. She didn't get any psychic impression from the information. The web had its own spirit, different even than that of most physical electronics. An urban animist once told her that the internet was exactly that: a net or web of threadlike ley lines with its own rules and its own spiritual vibration, a wholly human-made new thing. That guy claimed he could talk to the web itself, but he was also a squatter living in a yurt in someone else's backyard. Kelly didn't take him too seriously, but she had seen enough to believe that there were some web adepts capable of pulling those virtual "ley threads" just as a traditional animist might pull medicine from the ground or rain down from the sky.

Kelly Mun, to her great frustration, was not one of these adepts. To her, the web—and any information she got from it—had no smell. She had to do the leg work of investigating in the old-fashioned way to get a psychic impression. There was, however, a cloaked occult web to help dig past all the digital noise.

"The girl. Tonya. She follows a band up from Portland, goes to their show, takes an overdose of bardo . . . and then people see her body literally fall apart. Let's rule out good old-fashioned murder before we assume that a street drug made this woman break into pieces. Whoa"—Kelly pointed at the screen—"zoom in on the gore."

Critter enlarged the latest pic. A close look at the wounds, at least what the camera revealed, showed Kelly more of the strangeness Martinetti only hinted at.

"Look how clean those cuts are. They should be ragged. I doubt very much anyone could've had the time, strength, and swinging clearance to cut this woman apart that cleanly in a roomful of sweaty kids. And there's blood, but there should be more. A whole lot more."

Critter chewed his lower lip. "Well, I've never seen anything like this. Barring something unheard of, like time-stopping serial killers or invisible blades, I guess we're looking at witchcraft."

"Not quite. Alchemy. Let's assume it *is* the result of a drug overdose. If a street drug caused that, then we're looking at a fusion of magic and chemistry. Not our usual forte, but nothing about this case is usual. Martinetti said this shit has been on the streets for about a month. Why hasn't bardo done this to anyone else yet?"

"Maybe it has." They shared a moment of silence as they contemplated the implications. Then Critter sighed and took a pull from his iced latte. The straw sucked mostly air. "Okay, here's the weirdest part—"

"Weirder than a twenty-one-year-old breaking into pieces at the stroke of midnight in a packed room?"

"Touché. But here, someone swears this girl had only one arm when she walked in. There are two arms in the remains, a right and a left, and they look like they match. I don't like it, Kel. This just gets weirder and weirder. I'm not sure you should take this job."

Kelly grabbed her high-end, secondhand coat from the rack by the office door. "If you want your back pay, I absolutely should. Find everything you can on the hexweb while I'm gone." And with that, she was out the door, the soft tap of her cane fading down the hall.

The Deep was lousy with cops and onlookers. They swarmed like ants on carrion—though ants provide an essential function in an ecosystem. The journalists had already come and gone. Twelve hours after Tonya Williams's spontaneous disintegration, no one was sure whether to label this an act of terrorism, murder, or an occult incident. The press, predictable as ever, leaned toward the most sensational option.

The rain drifted more like a mist as Kelly scanned and sniffed the crowd for a perpetrator, returning to the scene. She leaned on her sturdy cane and closed her eyes. The city smelled like it always did, gray and powdery, like crumbling newspapers and smoke and dust. Today, under the usual urban notes that mixed with the more pleasant ones of Pike Place Market, Kelly smelled evil. Real evil—premeditated, calculated, and cruel.

Most people who did nasty things smelled like violence and fear but not outright evil. True evil smelled like something so deeply embedded that it would take months to purge it, like tumors growing in the marrow of bones. Today, the street in front of the Deep smelled like that, and of sadism. Like tears and bruises, like adrenalin and the bite of a whip.

Kelly suspected that Tonya's killer was still here. If she could get ahold of some bardo, she might be able to track a scent. Would anyone be stupid enough to linger at a crime scene while carrying drugs?

Of course, they would. This was Seattle.

Before the street sounds drowned it out, an overheard police radio confirmed that the bomb-and-drug-sniffing dogs had already been through. That was usually a dead giveaway. Most dogs didn't like the smell of magic; it disoriented them. Dogs usually backed off or ran outright from a site of witchcraft. Occasionally, they ran toward it like it was a peanut butter and bacon sandwich, tripping on their own dizzy paws.

Humans weren't much better. Most people couldn't reconcile the occult with their need to control and predict their own reality. Some people, mostly the atheists, were adamant that there was no such thing as magic. Those with a superstitious nature believed in it deep down, but it scared them, so they avoided talking or even thinking about it. In general, people just ignored the occult or explained it away. A few misfits—the psychics, the queers, the neuroatypical, and the natural-born witches—couldn't ignore it, so they often embraced it. Kelly and Critter were such misfits. So was Martinetti, it seemed.

In the paid parking lot on First and Pike, next to the Deep, Kelly found exactly the misfit she was looking for. Just to her right, a blonde woman said, "Am I free to go?"

An officer answered. "For now, yes. But stay available. We may need to call you in for more questioning."

The woman, more of a girl, shivered in the misty rain and pulled out her phone. Kelly came around behind her and saw she was ordering a ride.

"Miss, I'm so sorry to hold you up."

The girl turned but didn't take her eyes off her phone. "Yeah?"

Kelly said, "I'm here to make sure the police are treating everyone with respect and not adding to the trauma. May I buy you a cup of coffee?"

The girl looked at her for a long moment before bursting into sobs. She tucked her phone into her pocket and let Kelly touch her on the shoulder.

"Hey, you're gonna be okay. If coffee isn't enough, I can take you someplace else you can dry off and get warm. I know what this must look like. I'm here to help people like you. Survivors." Kelly hoped this girl didn't have a strong bullshit detector.

When the girl relented, Kelly brought her to the nearest coffee house and escorted her to the bathroom. The girl happened to know the key code by heart.

"It's just the zip code. Nine-eight-one-oh-one."

Inside, they cleaned her up. Kelly maintained her own cover story while also prompting the girl for as much information as she could get.

"I've been in your shoes." That wasn't a lie. "If you want to tell me what happened in there before the police detained you, feel free. Sometimes talking about it makes it easier—but not when they're interrogating you. I'm not interrogating you." That, on the other hand, was certainly a lie.

The girl continued crying. Through quick breaths, she choked out a horrifying story: "I-I was just there—to celebrate—New Years—and I was dancing, and I saw this beautiful girl—and I went up to her—"

Racking sobs interrupted her. Kelly gave the girl another handful of paper towels and consoled her. She calmed down enough to continue.

"And there was this guy behind her, and the girl looked at me, and I went over. And I kissed her, and then it was midnight, and while I was kissing her—s-s-she—"

The girl broke down again, and she leaned in for comfort. "Her fucking head just came off!"

No scent of deception or omission. Nothing to suggest she was anything other than a traumatized bystander. Kelly didn't pick up much of a clairolfactory impression from this girl—smelled like sweat and weed and an inoffensive armpit odor, but that was it.

The girl snuffled back mucus and swallowed. "Who did you say you work for again?"

Kelly felt a sharp pang about lying, like neuropathy of the soul. "Survivor Advocates. We're new. We do oversight of public services and make sure that victims and survivors in the system get treated with the same fairness as criminals. Oh, and my name is Casey Moon."

Kelly always had the ability to lie effortlessly and with charisma. She wondered if she were born with the skill, but it didn't really matter. And she only got better at it when she became a full-blown opiate addict, as addicts tended to be. Her aptitude for deception didn't decline at all once she got sober and started feeling her conscience again, but these days, she tried to use it to make the world a slightly less atrocious place.

"I'm Fern," the girl introduced herself. "Fern Callahan. That's my real name. People think I made it up to sound like a flower. But it's my name. Do ferns make flowers?"

Kelly said she didn't know. Fern dried her eyes once again and leaned away.

"So am I considered a victim in this situation? I'm not, like, a suspect, am I?"

Kelly dialed up the empathy but tried not to be maudlin. "The police consider you a witness. I consider you a survivor."

Fern relaxed a bit more. "Can we go get a table? I'd love a chai."

In the café, Kelly watched as Fern stress-ate a bag of chocolate croissants and ordered a second chai. In no time, the sugar and the caffeine hit her bloodstream, and Fern told Kelly everything.

"And I use vapor all the time. I didn't tell that part to the cops, but you know. It's harmless, right? Who ever died from vapor?"

Of all the popular street drugs, vapor was kid stuff. It was mostly just nitrous oxide with a little THC. Whippits and weed. It wouldn't even cause most people to blackout, let alone spontaneously dismember.

Kelly sipped an overpriced Americano. "I've never heard of anyone dying from it, Fern. Please know that you didn't do anything to hurt Tonya. Whatever happened was not your fault."

"Was that her name? The police wouldn't even tell me. Tonya . . ." She stared into her chai. "Thank you, Casey. That means a lot."

Fern stuffed her face again. Kelly watched the crumbs collect on the girl's breasts.

The trust was there. Kelly, playing the concerned and sisterly Casey Moon, could ask pretty much anything at this point.

"What about her arms?"

"Herv armvs?" Fern said around a mouthful.

"Yes, there was some confusion about Tonya's arms. It probably sounds rude to ask. I'm sorry. Truly. But I need to ask these things to make sure you're going to be okay."

Fern gulped down her tea and said, "She only had one arm. People saw what they saw, but I was right up against her. But people see weird things, you know? My uncle is a psychologist, and he told me that eyewitnesses are often wrong about what or who they saw. That's scary, isn't it? To think how many people have been sent to jail or worse. Oh my god. What if someone thinks they saw something incriminating? I swear to god I didn't do anything but kiss her and share my vapor cloud."

Fern looked like she might start crying again.

"I'm sure you're fine, honey." Kelly was almost positive that no one would try to hang any responsibility on Fern. There was nothing to hang, but that wouldn't stop some people from making pitiful attempts to punish her, trying to give themselves some kind of resolution. No, Fern wasn't the kind of girl you'd sue for wrongful death. She had great teeth and nice hands. Whatever vapor-and-free-love kick she was on, she still looked like a "nice" girl from a "nice" family.

She was nosey, though. "Did you survive something bad too, Casey? Is that why you use a cane?"

Kelly felt her leg tingling. "I've survived a thing or two. But no, I have neuropathy in my leg." The cane was handmade from cottonwood with a large burl at the top that served as a handle.

"Oh. What causes that?"

Without a beat, Kelly said, "Snake bite." She'd practiced this half-truth for the ones that like to pry.

"Huh. That sounds terrible." Fern gave Kelly a sympathetic nod and furrowed her eyebrows.

Kelly pressed her a bit harder. "So you're 100 percent sure Tonya only had one arm?"

"Yeah. Is this some kind of test? Like my memory is affected?"

Kelly felt the girl clamming up. "No, no, nothing like that. It's more of an exercise in healing."

That seemed to satisfy Fern. Kelly always found it remarkable how trusting people could be of her when she was pumping them for information. It was time to leave Fern alone before she caught on.

"Well, I gave you my card, and I have your number. I'll be in touch with you." She hadn't given Fern a card.

The hug wasn't as awkward as usual. Kelly kept her own cynical demeanor switched off and the sweeter "Casey" switched on. Fern was only the beginning of the day's work, and Casey was more than an alias. She was a damn good cover story.

Sometimes, to stop a big evil, you had to commit a tiny one.

On the bus, Kelly let her rational thoughts relax and dilate, letting the details connect however they would. She wrote down whatever came to her. Soon she was in a hypnagogic state, barely aware of what she wrote.

blonde girl vapor trail. black girl vapor. black pieces. moonlight. bardo. a fern is a flower, is not a flower. fern is in the bardo. fiddleheads and bardo. electric pentacles, electric bardo. pentacles in the bardo. pentacular chai. a tree of bardos. a fig tree. a sephiroth of trees. bardo doesn't grow on trees. no one likes a quitter.

She kept her pen moving. It was a bit of self-hypnosis, an autopilot trance that still maintained awareness of one's actions and surroundings.

blood and money. blood and bardo. Sophia Martinetti. money bardo. blood money bardo. black white and red. arrogant bitch Martinetti. crime and punishment Martinetti. bardo. Tonya and Sophia sitting in a tree fern. K I S S I N G fern. nothing stings like a fern. picked apart. dismembered. electric dismemberment. corpse pentacle. five fingers and one arm. a five-sided die. a dying star. a starfish growing back her arm.

Kelly brought her mind back into rational mode. She looked over what she'd written.

a fern is a flower, is not a flower. bardo doesn't grow on trees.

Those passages, besides sounding like pure Gertrude Stein, suggested that bardo wasn't plant derived. So it probably wasn't a narcotic. What the fuck was it then?

blood and money. blood and bardo. Sophia Martinetti. money bardo. blood money bardo. black white and red.

That didn't show her anything she didn't already know, but the words confirmed for her that Martinetti was absolutely involved more than she'd let on. Then there was that part at the end: *corpse pentacle. five fingers and one arm. a five-sided die. a dying star. a starfish growing back her arm.*

Was bardo a failed medical drug, something to stimulate tissue regeneration? It had the opposite effect in the end. The side effects on Tonya Williams were too dangerous to market to the public, but bardo must have some kind of euphoric effect. Why else would the club kids take it? The manufacturer might be pushing it on the street instead, trying desperately to turn profit from an expensive mistake.

It wasn't a bad lead. As an oracle, automatic writing wasn't the best, but like all divination, it clarified suspicions at the very least. It pulled knowledge up from the subconscious waters and into the airy world of conscious thought. It revealed to Kelly the things she didn't know she knew. But she still didn't know how much she didn't know.

Kelly would have to figure out how to interrogate Martinetti—probably by a direct confrontation. No "Casey Moon" tricks. Martinetti was as sharp as the business end of a scalpel, but she hid that behind her veneer of vanity and superficial haughtiness. She had her own tricks, which any clever and ambitious woman would have to cultivate in the macho empire of corporate elite. Her arrogance was likely as much a real weakness as it was a useful front. *Both/and.* Real people were messy like that.

Kelly shut her eyes, went back into the trance, and began drawing. When she came out of the automatic state, Kelly saw that she'd drawn the number five over and over again, though in three different forms: the Arabic numeral used in the Western world, the Chinese Hanja, and the Korean Hangul. Five, o, daseot.

She hadn't written Korean in years. She could barely do more than count in her father's language. He would teach her to speak it at random times, and then at others he would grow icy and ignore her when she asked for a lesson. Kelly always figured he was torn about his past and how much of it to bring with him into his new American family.

She knew next to nothing about her Korean family, save for what her father babbled in full blown dementia on his death bed. He'd been dead since she was 19, and she didn't care to remember him much.

She realized she'd missed her stop. She changed busses and headed back to the Deep.

Midday, the club stayed closed. The staff were likely shaken to their bones, and no bands were booked for the first of the year. The Silver Ash Cure had taken their bus and gotten the hell out of Seattle. The Electric Pentacle, however, stuck around to grieve.

Steam rose from a manhole cover next to the tour bus. Drunks and careless people got scalded by it all the time, but the city still used steam for heating since the gas explosions of the twentieth century. It was an urban hazard, and many complained, but everyone put up with it.

Through the billows of steam, Kelly saw a man leave the bus. It was the lead singer, Seth Agua.

"Hey!" she called.

He turned to look at her and nearly stepped into the venting steam.

"Watch out!" Kelly stepped forward to save him from the burn.

"Whoa. Thank you," he said. He smelled like bourbon and pain.

"You're Seth, right?"

"Hey, sweetie, I've had a real bad night. I don't have time for groupies right now."

Kelly looked into his bloodshot eyes. "Actually, that's what I wanted to talk to you about. I'm Casey Moon. From *Flinch Magazine*."

"No interviews right now," Seth said. "I need a coffee."

Kelly tried another tactic. "I have bardo."

Seth got aggressive. Kelly got ready to either de-escalate or fight it out. "I said leave me the fuck alone, bitch! I don't know you!"

He staggered away, off to become someone else's problem. Through the steam and the whiskey and the stink of tour bus living, Kelly smelled truth. Seth Agua had nothing to offer today. He probably had little to offer on most days.

Kelly calmed herself and knocked on the bus door. Finally, Gloria Hologram, the light-wave conductor, opened it and said, "You a cop?"

Kelly went through the routine again. Same character, different job. Casey had more careers than Barbie at this point.

"I'm Casey Moon. From *Flinch Magazine*? I was covering your show last night and wanted to follow up."

Gloria looked down at her. Gloria's spiked, snow-white hair blew in the breeze, and the blood-red tips of it made her look cartoonish.

"Gimme a sec." Gloria shut the door and opened it a minute later. "What the hell. Come on in."

Gloria was even thoughtful enough to give Kelly a hand climbing into the bus. Entering, Kelly saw the rest of the band scattered around the interior, most of them looking as bad off as Seth.

"Sorry, which magazine?" Gloria asked, dropping onto a couch. "And please have a seat."

"*Flinch*. The online version, not print."

The rest of them either stared at her or stared down.

"I know this isn't the best time. Thanks for letting me in."

One of them snorted. It was either the guitarist or the bassist. The two men looked alike in their promotional pics.

Kelly ascertained that the police had already questioned the whole band. She pressed on. "I was at the show last night. I wanted to give you all a chance to comment before the twenty-four-hour news media wears you down. I know they've been pestering you for hours."

"And just when they take a lunch break, you show up," said the guitarist. Or the bassist.

Gloria came to Kelly's defense. "No, this is good. I'm glad we can get some stuff online. The phones have been buzzing nonstop."

As if on cue, a phone clattered on the tabletop. They all jumped.

"Would you put that fucking thing in your goddamn pocket?" Gloria shouted. "Jesus. How many times do I have to ask you?"

The drummer grabbed it and stuck it into the pocket of her jeans.

Kelly kept quiet and let them show her the offstage dynamic. Kelly only had to listen, and the Pentacles would fill the silence.

Gloria was the one in charge here, despite the face time Seth Agua received as lead singer. It was also rumored that Gloria wrote all the music for every instrument, at least according to the scant amount of articles Kelly had time to read before strongarming the band into a slippery interview. The way Gloria Hologram held court on the bus confirmed Kelly's hunch that she was the real ringleader, and fortunately, she was itchy to talk.

"I mean, this shit happens sometimes," Gloria began. "You're doing a show, someone ODs or a fight breaks out and gets nasty. Or someone gets shot. Our fans are pretty chill, but like I said, shit happens."

The drummer, who went by Larva, jumped into the conversation. "It was horrible. One minute, it was a lovefest, and everyone was making out for New Year's. And the next, people were screaming and running, and people got trampled. Did anyone else die?"

Kelly fudged a believable answer. "No word yet. They're keeping people's names out of the media for now, but I hadn't heard of any fatalities other than the young woman."

Larva stood up. "It's witchcraft. That's the only explanation. We do rituals and shit on stage, but most of it's just show. I mean, I'm non-denominational pagan, so's Seth, but we play it up for the fans. I swear we didn't make her fall apart. That's some next level shit. Diabolism."

The bassist (maybe) said, "We don't know that. Don't be paranoid."

Kelly just let them go on. She hadn't expected to get much out of the others besides Gloria, but once Larva had her non-confessional outburst, the others were chiming in too. So far, no scent of lies, just medical-grade weed and a lot of booze. A hint of guilt in the air, but it smelled fresh and green, like survivor's guilt.

"If that was witchcraft," Gloria said, "it was way beyond anything I've ever seen. I've seen people raise a ghost or cure a fever, but I have never even *read about* someone just coming apart like a puppet."

"Ask me," said one of the men, "it's a mass hallucination. Or some kind of sick prank. The girl's dead, that's probably real, but the rest is smoke and mirrors. Like the whole arm thing. It just doesn't add up."

After the Pentacles slung a few more theories around, Kelly asked, "Do you think bardo was involved?"

"What?" Gloria said, the color draining from her already pale skin.

"Bardo. The drug she took. It's super underground, but it won't stay that way for long."

The other Pentacles looked nonplussed, but Gloria breathed hard. She smelled like that "under-scent," that strange note in the Seattle air that Kelly noticed this morning.

Gloria spoke in a stage whisper. "If I tell you something, something I've only told the cops, it has to be off the record, okay?"

Her bandmates stabbed their glances at her.

"You guys, someone died. At our show. In front of two hundred people. That's not the kind of thing you should keep secrets about."

"Casey" swore it wouldn't be published in the article. Technically not a lie.

Larva spoke up again. "That Tonya woman came around before the show, trying to get signatures or selfies and kisses or whatever. She asked us if we had any bardo. That's the first I'd ever heard of it, and I think that goes for everyone else here too."

Gloria hung her head beneath her shoulders. "I told the cops that we met her before the show, but nothing seemed weird about that. Usual fan stuff. They said nothing more about the bardo, so neither did I. Seemed like the cops hadn't heard of it either. You know how cops are the last to know anything."

Heads nodded all around the room. "So what is it?" Larva asked. "Bardo."

Kelly met the Pentacles' honesty with a lie. "I wish I knew, Larva. It's probably nothing. Kid stuff, like vapor." Then she added some truth, albeit strained through her cover story. "If *I've* never heard of it before today, it's probably a dead-end lead. It's my job as a journalist to know about these things."

"About that, Miss Casey Moon . . ." said the other one who was either the guitarist or the bassist. He cradled a smart phone in his hand. "I'm looking around the net, and I don't find you anywhere associated with *Flinch Magazine*."

Fuck. Maybe they'd fall for plan B, as cringe-inducing as it was, but it would help her get out of there unscathed.

"Well, not that it's everyone's business, but I'm transitioning. I don't use my dead name anymore, but it's on my old links. This is my first story since returning to work." She felt guilty immediately, but she had to do what she had to do.

"Asshole," Larva whispered. Kelly wasn't sure whether Larva was talking to her or to the accusing bandmate.

"Casey, I think you'd better go," Gloria said. She was catching on quickly now. "Don't put anything in your write-up about Tonya coming to the bus. If you do print it, I'll tell the cops you came around asking suspicious questions. They can figure out if you are who you say you are."

Kelly thanked them for their time and got the hell out. As she left, one of the men said, "And don't forget to download the new album!"

Back on the city bus, Kelly tallied her sins (so far) for the first day of the year:

- I nearly lost a client because I was late and didn't check the news.
- I killed Critter's plant.
- I took a dangerous job from a suspicious client.
- I messed with a traumatized girl's head to get information.
- I pretended I was trans to lie my way out of a problem and gain sympathy.

This year was off to a real banging start.

While she was at it, how long had it been since she talked to Brigid? She was embarrassed how many months, perhaps years, it had been. Beyond embarrassed, she was ashamed, and it made her put off asking Brigid for help. She added another offense to this list that only she cared about:

- I'm too ashamed to talk to Brigid when I need her.

Kelly tucked her self-loathing into the back of her mind and took her iPad out of her bag. She opened her cut-up app and typed in the automatic writing she'd made previously. She entered five for the degree of randomization. When the computer had done its job, the following cut-up text appeared:

black electric money tree Five fingers one likes a quitter. and one arm. bardo is a blood money blood and sophia money white punishment bardo. S I N. vapor bardo a Corpse flower. S I N G. a fig tree. of bardos. a fig tree. corpse pentacle. five fingers and electric bardo. Tonya picked apart. dismembered. electric dismemberment. picked apart. bardo flower, is not a flower.

The cut-up provided insights even more interesting than the trance-writing. Numbers, one and five. "Sin" and "sing," "corpse pentacle," "Tonya picked apart . . . electric dismemberment." All of that still pointed toward the Electric Pentacle, but their body language seemed like they weren't hiding anything. Kelly hadn't smelled a single lie among them either, which was pretty unusual for rockstars. She made a mental note that the Pentacles might be *too* clean, whatever that indicated, but that wasn't a lead yet.

Then there was the matter of the "corpse flower." That seemed too good, too familiar not to follow up. She ran a cursory search for the term and didn't need to go further.

Amorphophallus titanum. Or titan arum. The Sumatran corpse flower. *Bunga bangkai* in Indonesian. There were four in Seattle alone—two in the Volunteer Park Conservatory and two in the Tigris biomes—and those were just the ones displayed to the public. Private collectors might have others.

It was a big leap, bigger than usual for an investigation. The sense of doubt crept in.

Faker. Impostor.

She thought about Martinetti's words: *Glaring coincidences that lead nowhere. Barely tangential connections that make all the difference.* It sucked that Martinetti had more faith in Kelly than the detective had in herself. She took some deep breaths and calmed her mind.

This is what Martinetti is paying you double for, Kelly told herself. *Do your job. Take her money. Who cares if it's bullshit or real as long as the client gets their answers?*

Her phone buzzed. It was Critter.

"Hey, Kel. So I did some digging. I think we're dealing with Creole Vodou."

"Voodoo? In Seattle?" Nothing like that had come up in the automatic writing or the cut-up.

"Oh honey. It's everywhere. I dated this guy once, white as marble, and he used to go to a Vodou temple somewhere around here."

"Yeah? How'd that go?"

"Oh, he ghosted. Someone left a dead rabbit on his doorstep, which I guess is super bad, and he bugged out. Anyway, about the connection. Get this. There's a spirit in Vodou called Ti Kitha Demembre."

"Tiki Toddy Mamba?" The words smelled like sex and sweat.

"I'll text you the spelling. Anyway, I was digging around, and everything online says the exact same thing about her. Same words, same order. It's like there's an infinite loop of citation but no original source. Real weird. So it turns out she's actually fakelore. Ti Kitha is a real Vodou spirit, but this version of her is BS. It was conjecture made by some unprofessional researcher, but it caught on. Like *razbliuto*, which isn't a real Russian word, but English speakers think it is. You know people think anything published is true."

"Okay, at this point, I'm lost. What does fake Voodoo and fake Russian have to do with bardo and Tonya Williams and Electric Pentacle?"

"Never mind about *razbliuto*. As for the Vodou connection, you're absolutely gonna shit the bed when I tell you. She's a divided goddess. Dismembered. But *demembre* doesn't actually mean dismembered. It means, like, the family land and cemetery or something similar, but somehow, that became a false cognate, and now people think she's a dismembered love goddess just because the internet said so. There's another one like that, a real one in Hinduism, named Chhinnamasta. She might be the inspiration for Ti Kitha Demembre, intentional or not. Fakelore is weird."

Kelly took a moment to process the information dump. "So she's an internet meme that people assume is real. And she's a goddess in pieces. The connection here seems really flimsy."

Critter paused on the other end of the line and then said, "But that's what you do. You take flimsy connections and weird tangents and make it work. This is why I love working with you, Kel. You're a weirdo genius who can smell ghosts, and you solve cases with Dada cut-ups and tarot cards."

Kelly sighed and let the compliments sink in. "Thank you. I needed to hear that right now. I'm on my way back to the office. Keep digging, and I'll be there soon. Oh, also I need you to find everything you can on the Sumatran corpse flower, especially any here in Seattle."

"One more thing," Critter said.

"I'm listening."

"I think Tonya may not be dead."

Kelly pulled the phone from her ear and looked at it in disbelief—then put it back to her head. "She's in pieces, Critter. Her head was severed from her body. She's not in a coma. She's really, most sincerely dead."

"Oh, like that's the *weirdest* thing we've heard today. It's a hunch, but if I'm right, you can literally put her back together, and she'll come alive again. Ti Kitha Demembre is a sex and marriage spirit, at least in the fakelore meme. She represents the union of separate people into a single body. That longing for reintegration."

Kelly rolled her eyes and sighed loud enough for Critter to hear it through the phone. "I guess, then, you should find out where they took her remains. I'm not exactly the sneaks-around-the-morgue type of PI, Critter. I'll need a little more convincing. And even if, by some Catholic Voodoo miracle, she actually . . . resurrects? Even if that's the case, what do we do with her then?"

"We can cross that bridge when we get there. I'm telling you. The body wants to be put back together. That's how this urban legend works."

"Christ. Now she's Frankenstein's monster. This case gets weirder by the hour."

They both went quiet for several long seconds. Critter, as usual, spoke first. "What have we got to lose? Non-Linear Investigations doesn't exactly have a dignified reputation. We don't really have a reputation at all."

"We're already in over our heads. You know that, right?" Thinking of poor Tonya Williams, she regretted the choice of words immediately.

"I know, Kelly. But isn't that, like, your favorite place to be?"

COAGULA

Thursday, January 2

HOSPITALS SMELL WORSE THAN MORGUES. AT LEAST TO PSYCHICS. DEAD bodies are usually quiet since their ghosts rarely linger with them—that is, assuming the bodies have been moved from the site of death. A hospital, though, houses the dying and the living, most of them suffering or else they wouldn't be there. Even the nurses suffer, in ways unlikely for those working the morgue. People waste away in a hospital; many in the morgue never even saw their death sneaking up on them. A morgue, especially a forensic one, has a faint and prickly smell, like a trace of acid reflux. A hospital smells like that but mixed with pus and lymph and blood-letting steel, all churned in a bucket made of antibiotic death with a desperate bouquet of lilies floating on top.

Kelly counted her blessings that the police had delivered Tonya Williams to the morgue. She failed to connive her way in to see the stiffs last night, even with a bit of hoodoo. Instead, she went home and focused her attention on making an amulet to invoke Kali: black tourmaline, hematite, smoky quartz, and a garnet all bound up in copper wire. Not that Kelly had much traffic with Kali, but she was a tough motherfucker of a goddess and as good at chopping down obstacles as she was at protecting the helpless. Hopefully, the amulet would ground her, would focus and protect her.

In the morning, she asked Sophia Martinetti to pull some strings and get her past the staff and in to see the bodies, and Martinetti was only too happy to oblige. Kelly suspected the client also enjoyed Kelly's incremental loss of pride. A morgue wasn't exactly a bank vault.

Critter tagged along for on-the-spot research. Nothing beat having a cousin with a library science degree, a smart phone, and an insatiable appetite for the occult. He and Kelly now sat in a surprisingly comfortable lobby while they waited for the word to go in. It smelled like sadness but also relief. Why were there always potted ferns in places like this? Did they really do anything to pacify the living as they waited to identify the dead?

"Have I told you about the new guy I'm dating?" Critter's enthusiasm usually overtook his sense of tasteful timing.

"No, but you're about to. Cue the music . . ." She teased him like a big sister would, but she secretly liked to keep tabs on whomever her baby cousin was seeing this month.

"I met him on AtaBoy. The atavism app? He has gills—external, frilly ones like an axolotl, not like a fish. They're really sensitive, and he likes when I—"

"Enough!" Kelly said, putting her hands over her ears.

Critter stuck his tongue out at her and started looking up axolotls on his phone. Kelly made some notes in her moleskine.

"I'm just trying to make us look like normal morgue visitors," Critter said. "Whatever those look like. With your secondhand trench coat and your little moleskine journal? You might as well have a neon sign over your head that says, 'Private investigator, right here!' Not subtle."

"And you look like you're going to a radical faerie camping trip with your green eyeliner and big fat crystal necklace. But do I tell you how to do your job? No."

Critter's fallen smile perked up again. "Yes, you do. All the fucking time."

"Well, cheers to you and the axolotl guy. Let me know if you decide to keep him." Kelly's neuropathy had eased today. She didn't need her cane, though she kept it with her in case the leg acted up or she needed to crack someone's jaw. Hopefully, this case wouldn't come to that.

A small man with fluffy, salt-and-pepper hair emerged from a door next to the front desk. "Kelly Mun?"

She stood, and Critter just played with his phone. The attendant walked up to her and shook her hand.

"I'm sorry, Ms. Mun, but I don't have all the paperwork ready on my end." At that, Critter looked up from his screen. The man went on. "If you're not family of the deceased, we need to know your credentials for viewing the body. You understand."

"We're here on behalf of Sophia Martinetti," Critter blurted out. Kelly kept her gaze on the attendant's face, always ready for these little surprises.

"Oh. Sorry. I'm afraid she didn't provide us with paperwork." Kelly used a little charm. Leaning on the cane helped to give her an air of fragility that men often fell for. It was worth a shot.

Whether it was the name-drop, the cane, or something else, the attendant said to follow him. Kelly did, but Critter didn't get up.

"Hey, dingbat. You're on the clock. Get over here."

He rolled his eyes and scurried after her.

The attendant, who still hadn't given them his name, went through the spiel. "If you've done this before, you'll recall that we usually start with pictures to identify a body. The family is coming up from Portland today to collect her remains and affects, and after they recognize a picture or two of her tattoos, we'll release Ms. Williams's body. Since you're here on"—the attendant hesitated—"*official* business, we'll skip the photo identification. I know you're not here from the SPD."

He meant the Occult Crimes Division. A recent addition to Seattle PD. It had taken them long enough to take crimes of magic seriously.

"If you're with Martinetti, I assume this is for something more discreet. Plus, you don't dress like a cop."

"Told you," Critter said in a stage whisper. Kelly rolled her eyes and grunted. She fingered the amulet in her pocket.

"Make sure you wear fresh gloves. Do not remove anything from the body," the attendant went on. "The police may still call and decide to do a postmortem. They've changed their minds more than once about whether that's going to be necessary."

Was that Martinetti's doing as well? Kelly wouldn't put it past her. They entered the room that held Tonya's body. Kelly expected it to be chilly and dim. Instead, it was like a museum archive, sunlight streaming in through one window. There the young woman was, naked in six tidy segments on an examining table.

"I've never seen cuts this clean on any murder victim," the attendant said. "Did she fall into a machine or something?"

Kelly needed to get this guy out of the room. She glanced at Critter, who smirked and said, "We're not supposed to talk about it. Where are the gloves that Miss Mun needs to put on?"

The man turned his back to them, and Critter slipped a sachet of hot foot powder into the man's coat pocket. It worked. The attendant stayed only long enough to witness Kelly glove up and then excused himself.

"That was quick. What's in this batch?" Kelly asked Critter as she used an unsharpened pencil to prod gently at Tonya's areas of separation.

"The batch of hot foot? The usual. Salt. Cayenne. Chalk. Grave dirt. I added a sprinkle of blister beetle to see what would happen. Seems to be working so far."

Kelly continued tracing the wounds. The cuts were just as clean as they'd looked in the haphazard social media posts. Being right here, almost touching Tonya's remains, they smelled like beer and sex and hope. Like youth, like untainted optimism. But there was also an unmistakable note of that *wrongness* that Kelly had smelled throughout the city since yesterday.

"That guy better not die from your goofer dust, Critter."

Critter let out a sound between a *tsk* and a sigh. "He won't die, Kelly. He might cheat on his wife, assuming he has one. And they're monogamous. Whatever straight people are doing these days."

Kelly laughed and snorted. "You're lucky you're adorable and smart. So is there anything else from your research that you forgot to tell me?"

Critter rocked on the balls of his feet and stared at the sunlit window. "Forgot? Nope. But I have a new spell for us to try."

He pulled out a lime-green pocket bible. A blue cord bound it tight, and the knob of a key protruded, marking a page.

"Book and key? You're gonna do book and key on a dead body?"

"It's super common in Jamaica, where Tonya's grandma is from. Probably other places too. Why not try?"

"Why not? Because it's a spell for finding thieves, not for gleaning info from a dead body. And because it's not our spell. Who knows what spirits you might offend."

"Says the lady making Kali amulets. Am I right or not? Magic doesn't have time for political correctness. Deities want to be remembered and worshipped. They take all kinds. You think spirits have time for our human bullshit?"

Point taken. He went on. "I adapted the spell. And as I told you, I don't think she's actually dead. I think she's just . . . dormant."

"Dormant?" Kelly gazed at the window as if surrendering to the gods for help. "Fine. Let's try it before your hot foot powder wears off and we get caught."

Critter did his little happy dance, which he did every time he tried out a new spell. Kelly imagined that if he had a musical theme it would be Peter's theme from *Peter and the Wolf.*

He suspended the book over the body, holding it by the knob of the key.

"Wait. What do we do if she wakes up?"

"Keep her away from Sophia Martinetti, I would think." Critter took a deep breath. He began: "By Saint Peter, by Saint Paul, by the Creator who made us all, Sophia Martinetti took this life."

Nothing happened. Kelly raised an eyebrow.

"Okay," Critter said. "I'm satisfied that Martinetti didn't intentionally cause this."

Kelly shook her head. "Whatever. I'm the investigator. You're the librarian. Keep going."

"By Saint Peter, by Saint Paul, by the Creator who made us all, Fern Callahan took this life." Again nothing.

He tried it using Electric Pentacle, Silver Ash Cure, and even bardo. Zilch.

Kelly grew antsy. "Are you sure this 'adapted' spell can even work?"

"Wait. Here's the moment of truth." He closed his eyes and inhaled. "By Saint Peter, by Saint Paul, by the Creator who made us all, this life was never taken."

Kelly jumped as the bible turned 360 degrees around the axis of the key.

"Shablam!" Critter said, dancing again. "Who's the baddest bitch? Huh? Say it with me!"

Kelly snatched the book and tucked it into her coat. "Shhh! Come on. We don't have time for peacocking."

They both hesitated, despite Kelly's urgency. "Okay, let's test the rest of your hunch."

Critter gloved up, and they both arranged the body, so the gaps were closed with a firm hand.

"Don't grind the joints!" Kelly said.

They stared at Tonya's dead body. Nothing happened. Then they heard approaching footsteps in the hall outside.

"Fuck! What now?" Critter backed away from the body.

"Which arm was it?" Kelly heard the footsteps grow louder, their pace steady.

"What?"

"She has two arms here on the gurney. We have to separate the arm that she lost before she died. The one Fern swore was missing."

Critter sprang back into position at the remains. "The right one!"

They pulled the right arm away from its shoulder. Again, nothing happened. "No, the left! The left!"

With a horrible, sticky sound, they got some space between the left arm and the body. The arm shriveled and then melted, bones and all, into a trace of tarry stuff.

Tonya Williams sat bolt upright and screamed.

Getting out of the morgue took even more effort than getting in. The attendant ran in at the sound of Tonya's scream, and he fainted at the sight. When Critter brought him round again, the man ran out of the room and called the police. Kelly made the executive decision not to run, which would've made everything worse.

The SPD wanted to examine Tonya and question everyone present, and they were already on the way. Without adopting the Casey Moon alias this time, Kelly went into action with her training in psychological first aid.

After calming Tonya and assuring her she'd be okay, Kelly and Critter found a hospital gown for her to wear. She still trembled, whether shivering with cold or exhaustion. When the attendant returned, he insisted on being there, but the sachet in his pocket continued to pull his attention out of the room. While the man was distracted, Critter whipped out a credit card and scraped up the gunk left behind by the phantom arm. He lured the man outside and signaled to Kelly that he was leaving and would call.

It would be a tight interview, but Kelly needed to do a little questioning before the cops could swoop in and really fuck everything up. Kelly calmed herself first, presenting motherly care for the girl. "Tonya, do you know where you are?"

Tonya sipped water from a paper cup. "The hospital?"

"Not yet. You're in a safe place near a police station. But you're not in trouble. Do you know what day it is?"

Tonya trembled and took another sip. "January 1st."

"Close. It's the second. You were in a coma for a day or so. I think you had a bad reaction to some recreational drugs. And again, you are not in trouble. You are not a criminal. Do you understand?"

Tonya nodded. Kelly smoothed her hand along Tonya's shoulders and continued. "I'm not a doctor, but I think you'll be okay now. We'll get you checked out and make sure there's no"—she hesitated, not wanting to make claims on which she had zero basis—"permanent damage. If you can, will you tell me the last thing you remember?"

Tonya stopped shivering. "Um. I was at the Deep for the Pentacles' show. And I was dancing. There was a girl in front of me and a guy behind me. I felt weird, and I guess I passed out. Did someone drug me and then . . .?"

Kelly synchronized her breathing to Tonya's and slowly brought it down again with Tonya following. Nifty trick, like a contagious yawn.

"No. I don't think you were sexually assaulted. We're still figuring out what happened, but there's no evidence of that. Do you remember anything else?"

Tonya closed her eyes. "I remember dreaming while I was . . . out. The dream kept repeating, like I had a fever or something. Just the same thing over and over with little changes. I was in this big empty place. Full of fog. And I was walking on cold water, like a lake, and no one else was around. I ran around and around on the water, looking for anyone, anything. Then I was in the water, but I wasn't drowning. I was swimming. And as I swam, I realized I had both my arms again, and I thought I was in some kind of heaven, but I was alone. It can't be heaven if you're alone, right? God is with you, and so are the ancestors. Right?"

That sounded a lot like *the* Bardo—the real one, not some mock-up drug. Tonya didn't wait for Kelly to respond.

"I saw the lights, like glowing moons in the water, and I thought I could come back if I swam into one. I tried, but it didn't work."

Kelly clenched her teeth and said the most comforting thing she could think of. "Well, you're awake now. Your soul is in your own body."

Tonya finally burst into tears of grief and relief. Kelly held her while she cried—and kept warning herself not to get emotionally involved, but what else could she do? Fern Callahan was sweet and easy to manipulate without causing further damage, another clueless witness who didn't understand what she saw. But Tonya Williams had just returned from the dead. This was a whole different kind of trauma.

Critter, ever the data whiz, texted Kelly: *We got here just in time. Her family has been informed she's alive and they're already en route.*

Good. That was what the girl needed, not to be prodded by cops and doctors. She told Tonya, "I'm so sorry, but there will be other people here very soon. They're not going to be gentle with you like I am. They're going to ask you a lot of questions, trying to find out why this happened to you, and they'll probably move you to a hospital to make sure you're okay. Your family is also coming up from Portland. I hope that's a good thing."

Tonya sniffled. "Yeah, that's good. I want my grannie."

Kelly decided that it would be too much at this point to tell her that she was, for all intents and purposes, dead and mutilated until five minutes ago. Just let the girl cry it out now and start to feel a little bit stable.

"I'll try to come visit, and I'll try not to let them make you feel worse than you already do. Remember, you have rights. They can't keep you here if you don't want that."

She gave Tonya the protection amulet, realizing now why she'd made it in the first place. It was never meant for Kelly.

That was when the officers showed up. A tall man, Somali or Ethiopian she guessed, walked in and locked eyes with Kelly. "Kelly Mun?"

Another officer came in behind him and approached Tonya slowly—thank god they sent a woman. It was no guarantee of gentility, but at least they didn't send the bulls to pick out the china.

Kelly nodded to the male officer, who told her, "I'm Detective Aweke. Occult Crimes Division."

The detective questioned her a bit while his colleague spoke softly with Tonya. Kelly could tell that the lady cop was giving Tonya softball questions, and she could smell that ozone scent of omission. These officers knew some things that Kelly didn't.

Aweke was still questioning her when the other officer helped Tonya stand and walked her out.

Kelly waved and said goodbye. "Stay strong!" she shouted after the women as they walked out the door. She was surprised how much she let Tonya's case get to her. Then she turned her full wrath onto Detective Aweke.

"So. Are you real PD or just an agent for Martinetti?"

He smiled. "You're the one who's supposed to think in nonlinear terms. This is a *both/and* situation."

"This is what she does then? Organized criminal occultism? Is that her 'research and investment' business? She swore she wasn't mafia."

"What she does is none of our business. She pays well and on time. I very much doubt she's somewhere sacrificing little unbaptized babies to Moloch. Just collect the money. You'll sleep better."

"So what do *you* do then, Detective Aweke? What kind of dirty work does she pay you to do?"

"Now that we both know what we're doing here, feel free to call me Julian." He reached into his jacket. For a moment, Kelly thought he was pulling a weapon, and she got ready with her cane. Aweke rolled his eyes when he saw her tense up. What he presented to her were photographs.

They were photographs of Kelly herself.

"For one thing, Miss Mun, she pays me to find people like you. I've been surveilling you for a few weeks. I'm surprised you didn't smell it."

Martinetti had almost said as much to her already. *Sloppy,* she thought. *Get your shit together, Kel.*

"And when it comes to dirty work, you'll be disappointed to hear that you're the one doing it, not me. All I do is unlock, gather, and relay information. I create leaks. In fact, I'm the one who arranged for you to have access here. I don't fancy going into morgues and poking dead women until they wake up."

Kelly tightened her fist on the head of her cane. Was everyone working for Martinetti as salty as the woman herself?

"If I were you, Kelly, I'd be grateful." Aweke launched into his power trip. "I *let* your cousin slip out. I let you *in*. And I'm letting Tonya Williams go with her family. No harm will come to her. At least, not from Martinetti. I'm sure that woman gave you her famous 'I pay people off because killing them is too much work' speech, yeah? She loves that little monologue. To my knowledge, she's never had an innocent killed, let alone some girl who just woke up from an alchemical coma or whatever the fuck that was."

It smelled true, and there was a whiff of something extra. Sometimes Kelly could smell things like they were symbols, the way a lie smells like halitosis. Other times, she could smell impressions of things that weren't present but had been in the air. The extra note hanging around Aweke didn't smell symbolic at all. It smelled like sex—but not recent. She hoped he wasn't imagining her that way.

He kept right on talking. "I've known Martinetti for a long time. She did once have a real piece-of-shit guy tortured and interrogated, but trust me, he deserved it. He was sex trafficking underage kids. The testicles of a rapist can be used in some very powerful conjuring, and he won't be needing them anymore."

He was letting her know not to fuck with him or Martinetti, which she already knew. Cops always liked to state the obvious. Kelly ground her teeth and thought about what to say. She decided to use the detective as an ally, not a friend.

"So if we're both paid to do the same thing—more or less—are we competing? Shouldn't we be working together?"

Aweke smiled. He was handsome despite being a power-tripping dickhead.

"Quid pro quo, as the cannibal said. What've you got on bardo that you think I don't already know?"

Kelly sat in the back seat of the Garuda and went over her notes. Martinetti told her on the morning call to just bill for any expenses like travel, and it was nice to go a bit posh for a change and give her leg a break. No more bus stops.

The Garuda app was like any other car service, but they gave stock to drivers. Their logo was Garuda himself, a happy winged god with the head of a bird. In Hinduism, he was a living vehicle for a superior god. That was an odd ego stroke for the passengers.

She thought about scraping together enough capital to buy their stock—or to quit detective work and drive for them. Come to think of it, Martinetti probably had stock. Everything Kelly billed, she knew, would be written off. She needed to take advantage of this new client without wearing out her welcome.

"Whatever the market will bear," Detective Aweke had said. Street drugs didn't get the kind of bean counters that Big Pharma had. Part of the bardo "rollout," as he called it, would involve seeing how much the user would pay. Since no one knew whether it was addictive, that price was probably still low. He knew a lot about the drug trade, possibly from undercover work, possibly from dealing. Or maybe he was just a good, clever cop.

Clever, at least.

She'd been able to needle some info from Aweke, but it wasn't much. Mostly confirmation of her suspicions, which was still something she could use. If he was telling her the truth—and it smelled like the truth—Seattle PD had also been unable to get a sample of bardo. The most they had were rumors and dead ends. Tonya was the best and only real lead, but she'd soon get lost in the bureaucracy. It would probably take them six months just to correct the public record of her non-death.

Detective Aweke said that the FBI had nothing and perhaps hadn't even heard of it yet. Aweke knew it was on the street, and he believed it was being manufactured and tested in Seattle, but Tonya's remains were the first physical evidence. And now that evidence was breathing and talking and bundled in a blanket at Swedish Hospital or Harborview, getting ready to leave the city entirely.

"We can't hold her," he admitted. "There is no procedure on the books for arresting, detaining, or questioning a resurrected murder victim. No one's ever seen a dead girl walk out of the morgue. She doesn't even have scars from the incident. It's like it never happened. We're hoping her bloodwork will show us something. Anything."

He also admitted that he'd ruled out everything other than magic. SPD sent in the occult detectives because they had absolutely nothing else. The lack of evidence itself was evidence: something was cloaked, and it was being cloaked hard. Cloaking spells always left a hole, a vague silhouette of distortion where the hidden bumped up against the unobscured. You had to look for the hole, not the quarry. Any concentration on the quarry would only result in vertigo. The more intense the focus, the more disorienting the results, like sliding on a slick floor and catching oneself—but that disorientation could also be used to detect a cloak. It took a master of the craft to cloak the cloak just enough that no one would notice it.

Aweke suspected that whatever was happening with bardo was happening just out of sight or even in plain sight. They chased something solid yet invisible, only knowing it was there by the shadow it cast. Unfortunately, any decent cloaking spell would absorb the needed light and leave no shadow.

It wasn't a lot to go on, but if nothing else, Kelly now knew Martinetti had cops on her payroll. Julian Aweke might even be a double agent, undercover and infiltrating Martinetti's clandestine whatever-it-was she did all day. Or a triple agent, also working for whoever was testing bardo on the street. Or—

Relax, she told herself. *Look at the data. Don't invent a narrative where there isn't one.*

She brought her attention back into the present. At least the driver wasn't talking. She disliked the chatty ones. *Just do your job. Be the chariot you're paid to be.*

The car smelled like a nice, clean car and the driver like a good, honest soul. A khanda dangled from the rearview mirror. So he was Sikh. Did they have Garuda in Sikhism? Maybe this was data worth entering into the cut-up generator. Worth looking up, either way.

She opened up the little pocket bible that Critter had used for the book-and-key spell. That was a pretty badass little cantrip, she had to admit. The marked page was Exodus 20, the commandments. The one for murder and the one for stealing were nearly consecutive, 20:13 and 20:15 respectively, and adultery at verse 14 between them. She made some notes, not quite auto-conscious but definitely free association:

Exodus 20:13. 20:14. 20:15. 2019. Midnight 2020. Gateways between years, between decades. Is Tonya the gate? Is bardo the gate?

Military time. 8:13–8:15PM. 23:59 on 12.31.2019. Adultery holds the space between murder and theft. It steals the heart and murders love.

Garuda is the chariot of the gods. Garuda wields the khanda. Am I the khanda? The khanda cuts open the veil. Opens the gateway.

She did some numerology with the bible verses: 20:13 added up to six, the Lovers card in the tarot. That was curious. The Lovers represented choices and relationships, especially the choices that meant leaving behind childish needs and embracing adulthood. That sounded like a "gateway" for sure. It also corresponded to what happened to Tonya and this fakelore Ti Kitha Demembre spirit: union of separate souls into one by sex and marriage and mingling the flesh. The Lovers were in the major arcana, so they meant much deeper things than their title suggested. Three of Swords was always grief. Seven of Wands was pretty much always valor. But the Lovers could be any number of things.

That meant that 20:15 would be eight. Strength, sometimes switched with Justice. Too much esoteric static there, and her intuition told her to take a different route.

In between those two, Exodus 20:14 added up to seven, the Chariot. Of course it was the Chariot. Not just travel but a parade of triumph, and the verse was about adultery. Adultery and the Chariot. The gateway between Murder and Theft. Lovers and Strength. She could smell that she was onto something promising. It was like chocolate and gold and the spreading shoots of plants. Fiddleheads. She made her final notes as the car pulled up to the Tigris Biomes on 7th Avenue.

She tipped the driver 100 percent on a relatively small fare. Bonus for not chatting. It was Sophia Martinetti's money; let her put it back into the economy at the worker's level.

Tigris Inc. was slowly taking over the South Lake Union neighborhood, absorbing property and people alike. The company relocated their corporate office from Saudi Arabia to Seattle only five years back, but like creeping ivy, the company bought up one property after another. The longtime locals resented this deeply with a curious mix of anti-capitalist leftist sentiment and old-fashioned racist xenophobia. For all Kelly knew, Martinetti was a high stakeholder in the company. She didn't come up on many of the searches that Critter ran, and that could only be intentional.

The Biomes were very new: big glass domes out of some utopian 1990s dream of self-contained ecosystems, but finally sustainable as a commercial organism. Some people called them the Bubbles or the Domes or the Glassholes, but most commonly the Pods. Seattleites joked that these hybrid office-leisure-greenhouses were the place that Tigris grew all their pod people. The Tigris employees did have a creepy loyalty to the company. It reeked of secrets, but it didn't smell like bardo or anything else about this case.

The "corpse flower" reference in the cut-up she ran yesterday kept nagging at her. She needed to check out the lead. There weren't a lot of those around, and outside the tropics, they only grew in tended greenhouses.

She walked into the warmth of the pods, which were somehow less humid than the cold, rainy street outside. She paid for a ticket and joined a tour group. The tour guide's name tag read, "Shiv K.," and under that, "Varanasi, India."

Shiv led the group around the tourist-accessible areas of the greenhouse. Some of the flowers, likely the poisonous or psychotropic ones, gave Kelly a bit of contact high and made her momentarily lightheaded. Star lilies and dogwoods always did that to her. Nothing psychic or magical there, but she did get a mild psychic impression if she got too close to something like salvia or datura. Ironically, cannabis smoke had barely any effect on her.

The Tigris Biome concentrated so many unfamiliar plants into such a small area that it made her woozy. Through the dizzying perfume, Kelly's clairolfactory abilities became dampened. She risked the side effects and took a deep whiff—the flowers had the psychic charge of being merely ornamental, not used to influence minds or obfuscate secrets. Not intentionally.

The guide explained how he came to be recruited by the company and flown here from Varanasi to start his career. Mr. K. was apparently a wunderkind with organic technologies and cultivated a specialization in bamboo. He probably made at least six figures a year, maybe even seven, Kelly reckoned.

"I volunteer to give tours because it brings me pleasure," he informed the tour group. "I like to meet people and share with them my infatuation with plants." He showed them some of the flowers and trees native to his home: banyan, monkey puzzle, hibiscus. He named others that he'd never seen in person before moving to the US: melaleuca, aloe, strawberry.

The tour group wound its way up the spiraling floors. Much of the Biome was off-limits to anyone outside of the Tigris in-crowd. Kelly could pick up the faint scents of many bizarre and clandestine things going on belowground, like a botanical version of Willy Wonka's chocolate factory, but none of them had the stink of bardo or abject evil about them. Greed and exploitation, yes. But pure malice? No.

Although they weren't allowed into the actual office spaces, Kelly observed plenty of Tigris employees taking their tea and coffee on benches beneath cascades of flowers and carefully sculpted living trees. Shiv explained that the office spaces themselves were airlocked, keeping the humidity out. He kept using the word *hybridize*.

"—so Tigris decided to hybridize more than just our software. We've also hybridized work and leisure into the Biomes. Next, we want to pioneer sustainable electronics using bamboo and other plant-based materials to replace plastics and metals, hybridizing the biological with the digital. We're working on making a neural network from bamboo fiber. Artificial intelligence that is not artificial at all."

Jesus, Kelly thought. *Next they'll be cultivating triffids.*

"We also have our coastal and offshore laboratories for aquatic botany, which I believe is the real future. Power the world with the sea. Light it with bioluminescent algae. Clean the air with free-floating super kelp."

It was a sexy pitch. He delivered it with all the enthusiasm of a zealot, and Kelly didn't smell any ulterior motive. He continued: "The Tigris corporation grew from the silicon sands of the desert. We crave the splendor of the forest and the jungle. This is the future of corporate culture. I go to work in a tree house. Perhaps you will one day as well."

The tourists ate it up like hibiscus sorbet. They clapped as he led them to the obligatory gift shop. Kelly had to admit to herself that she was taken with Shiv's speech as well, entranced by the mélange in the air and this man's botanical futurism. He'd make a very good contact on future cases.

It wasn't until she stood in front of the tiers of waxy, overpriced succulents that she remembered why she came here in the first place. There were two corpse flowers in here, according to Critter. She still had to check the Volunteer Park Conservatory for the other one and then have Critter dig up any private collectors in the area. Hopefully she'd get lucky and find whatever it was here that would connect to the next lead.

She approached Shiv just outside the gift shop. A misty waterfall behind him made for an excellent photo op but shitty conversation. Kelly almost yelled, "Excuse me, Shiv? I'm Casey. I was wondering, if you have some time before the next tour group, could you show me the corpse flowers? I missed them."

Shiv said something, and between his Varanasi accent and the waterfall, Kelly couldn't make it out. He gestured to another spot along the path. "I said it would be my pleasure, Miss Casey."

He led her to a spot off the usual path but still accessible. A sign read, "*Amorphophallus titanum*, corpse flower, Sumatra." The taxonomy translated to "giant shapeless cock." Botanists were a fun bunch.

Laminated pages hung by a key ring from a branch, and they detailed various facts about the plant and some pictures:

"Also known as bunga bankai in Indonesian. Not to be confused with *Rafflesia arnoldii*, the parasitic giant padma or 'monster flower,' also found in Indonesia."

In bloom, it looked like a gigantic calla lily but with a skirt of maroon instead of white. The spadix—the obelisk of flowers in the center—looked more like a long hoagie roll than a phallus, but no one asked her to name the damn thing.

All of this imagery came from the plastic pages dangling from the tree branch. The corpse flowers themselves were squat little green and brown things. Terribly disappointing.

"You just missed her," Shiv said. "She bloomed last July. I'm afraid that Putricia won't bloom again for several years. We hope that Elvira will bloom this summer or next."

"Putricia? The flowers have names?" Kelly sniffed them, but there was no offensive odor.

Shiv laughed. "They don't stink unless they're in bloom. Yes, they all have names. It is the fashion for every conservatory to name the bunga bangkai. The ones in Volunteer Park are named Wednesday and Pugsley. They are usually named like—how would you say it—kindergoth? Like for morbid children."

Kelly could smell wrongness now, but it wasn't coming from the corpse flowers. Was it coming from Shiv?

"Is there any folklore about them? Any magic or gods associated with them?"

Shiv squinted and gave a slight headshake. "That is something I do not know. You would have to ask someone more knowledgeable than myself."

That wasn't likely, as Shiv was doubtless a certified genius, even among the Tigris crowd. She kept up the charm a little longer so that he'd remember her if she needed his expertise.

These flowers were a dead end. She'd check in with Critter on the way to Volunteer Park.

"If you like folklore, I could tell you a story about this one," Shiv told her, guiding her to a nearby tree. This one had a sign that read, "*Bombax ceiba*, red silk cotton tree."

"This is the shalmali tree from India. Also called a kapok. It is used in traditional Ayurvedic medicine to treat all kinds of things: inflammation, fever, skin disease . . . impotence." His brown cheeks blushed.

Boner trees and shapeless cock flowers. Things were beginning to connect a little. Kelly smelled that promise smell, the gilded chocolate and fresh shoots. "Impotence, huh? What other stories are there about this tree? Anything from the *Rigveda*?"

"The tree is a residence of Garuda, the eagle. Vishnu rides on his back."

There it was. The coincidence that could mean nothing or everything. Kelly prodded Shiv for more. "You say that Vishnu rides on Garuda's back?"

"Yes, Garuda is his chariot."

That cinched it. "Thank you, Shiv. Too bad the corpse flowers aren't blooming yet."

Shiv blushed again. "Yes. It is too bad."

She shook his hand and tried to tip him. He refused, and she remembered that he didn't need her pocket cash. He asked her to put the money into the wooden coffers at the exits, but fat chance of that happening. Tigris, Inc. could afford to save the Amazon rainforest without her. They could afford to *buy* the rainforest, and a quick search on her phone indicated that the company already owned swaths of it.

Cheers to more pod people, she thought and made her way back to the gift shop. She decided to wander the racks and see if she spotted anything noteworthy. All she found was a novelty bottle of Putricia's Corpse Flower Perfume, which on closer inspection was actually a durian cologne. Nice gag gift for the missus.

Her phone buzzed. Not a text but a call from an unknown number. She answered.

"Kelly? It's Julian Aweke. We've found another body. I think it's bardo related. You really need to come see this."

"Shit. Already? Is it like the last one?"

"Not much like the last one at all, actually. White male, possibly teenager. Train hopper, from the look of him and where he was found."

"Is he in pieces?"

There was a pause while someone shouted in the background of Julian's phone. Then he said, "No, this one's in one piece. Hanged."

"That doesn't sound very magical to me. Does it look like a ritual killing?"

"Kelly, I know how this sounds, but it's easier if you just come see. It's difficult to believe if you don't see it for yourself. I'll text the address."

Another Garuda driver brought her down to a warehouse in SoDo. It wasn't the hip strip, where fashionably dilapidated storefronts sold "designer" furnishings, which hadn't been updated since the Bauhaus heyday. SoDo wasn't a Deco District or even a gentrified gayborhood, but it was what Seattle could scrape together from an overabundance of repurposed wood.

The crime scene was nothing like the buildings on the main drag. It was off the beaten path, though only a short walk from it. This was a true bashed-in warehouse: a hanger for small planes or train service or, most likely, a king's ransom in coal. Anything valuable had been stripped long ago. All but abandoned, it made it a perfect place for rail kids and oogles to squat on the way in or out of town.

It was challenging to establish much of a pattern between the two victims, just as Aweke said. This scene even smelled different. Tonya was middle class, and she had disintegrated in the middle of a crowd at a popular concert venue. This young man, yet to be identified, was found alone in an empty warehouse. He certainly had the traveler look to him—denim clothes held together with duct tape, pins, and sewn patches, not stylishly "distressed" but actually distressed. Like the runaway kids who hung out on University Ave. He had a sleeping bag and backpack full of portable belongings, reinforcing the rail kid story. He was someone Kelly's mom might've called a "hobo."

He was not in pieces. He dangled in midair, swaying just a bit, his head at a broken angle. As if a dead anonymous kid wasn't enough, there was the matter of the rope that hanged him.

There was no rope. He just floated in midair, swaying and turning, a ghost made of flesh.

"Think you can bring this one back to life, Miss Mun?" Julian sneered. His face held nothing but hatred for whoever did this.

SPINES

Friday, January 3

KAY, LET'S GO OVER WHAT WE HAVE."

Kelly and Critter sat in her office, leaving the door open on the off-off-chance that a client would walk in as Martinetti did.

Critter slurped his iced coffee. His eyes were bleary, but the lids twinkled with green and gold glitter. "So there is nothing—not a damn thing—on the hexweb about bardo. It's not on the rest of the dark web either, which is where the drug trade hangs out. I checked on Tonya. She's safe in Portland with family. She still remembers nothing but the bardo dream between her solvé and her coagula."

"Is that what we're calling it?" Kelly asked. She looked at the photos of Tonya's dismembered form. Critter's hunch had been correct though: the woman had only been in stasis until they fit her back together.

"What else would we call it? You said this is alchemy. She got *dissolved* into parts and then *coagulated* whole and alive again. As above, so below. Amirite? Do you know anything about alchemy?"

Kelly rolled her eyes. "That's what I have you for. We've been over Tonya's case enough. Did you get back the chemical profile on that stuff we scraped up when her arm dissolved?"

Critter made an "emoji face," exaggerating gritting teeth. "Sorry, Kel. I'll get it out today. I promise."

Kelly let out the kind of sigh reserved for waiting for a bus. "What lab are you sending it to?"

"Okay, so hear me out . . ." Critter stood up and started pacing.

Here we go, Kelly thought.

"So you know my friend Harriet? Local Salish, pink hair, light-skinned, big bodied?"

Kelly had no idea who Critter described. She cocked her head and blinked.

"Okay, so you don't know her. Anyway, she's working on her PhD in biochemistry at UW, and she's already working for a private company. I was thinking we should go to her first. She can look at it from both the toxicology angle and the physiological, she has access to multiple organizations' lab tech, and most importantly, she'll probably do it for free."

Kelly perked up. "So then what are you waiting for? Make it so, doofus. And now the homeless kid. Aweke is still working on identifying him. He said he'll leak info to me when he can get anything useful—"

"Did you tell him to give you the esoteric stuff too? The stuff that doesn't look useful?"

Kelly sighed again. "Yes, Critter. Thank you for double-checking."

He stopped pacing and sat in a chair, cross-legged, fidgeting with his knees. "Okay, cool. Just making sure."

"Let's take another look at the data. What do we know, and what do we think we know? We know the kid is dead—"

"Tonya wasn't dead."

"—and we assume his death is magic-related. The spectral noose, the levitation, or whatever it was. The smell of magic at the scene. Magic was there, and we can assume magic killed him. We know we didn't find bardo—or any illegal substances—at the scene. Nor did we find any talismans, gris-gris, hexes, etc. Like the Tonya Williams scene, the absence of a clear cause of death is more glaring than any actual evidence."

Kelly rubbed her leg. The neuropathy was better today but never entirely gone. It interfaced with her psychic abilities through some gift of neurological magic. If it ever stopped hurting entirely, that would be a warning. Every moment her leg tingled, even a little, meant she was safe.

"Your Vodou hunch had been right, Critter. Does the new one remind you of anything Vodou-related?"

Critter got up again. Kelly wasn't sure if his pacing was an unconscious habit or Critter's way of feeling like Sherlock Holmes. Both, most likely.

"I've been thinking a lot about that. Norse Odin is the best-known hanged god. I mean besides Jesus—but I don't think he's involved here. Odin is the most obvious lead, but I don't think it fits. I think there are some Mayan and Yucatan legends around hanging gods. There are gallows spirits in some branches of Vodou. Shango, the thunder spirit, is Yoruban. Also found in Haitian Vodou like Ti Kitha Demembre. Shango also shows up in Brazilian Candomblé and Cuban Santería. You gotta go really deep into the hexweb to find much on those traditions. The Yoruban legends say Shango hanged himself, or else he was pulled up to heaven by a spiritual chain. That connects him to Mary Immaculate and her ascension."

"What about Baron Samedi? Or one of the other Vodou barons?"

"Nah. General death spirits and healers. Cemetery gods. Not much hanging iconography for them. Crossroads and gallows are connected, but you're more likely to find Eshu around the gallows than the Baron."

Critter's info dumps made her head spin sometimes. He would get manic in his research and overshare.

"All of which is to say—no. But remember, Ti Kitha Demembre isn't an actual Vodou spirit. She's a meme and a mistranslation. I think that's what we should be looking at: fakelore, not folklore. Less Shango and Baron Samedi, more Slenderman. That's the hunch I've got. As of right now anyway."

Kelly knew his hunch could change at a moment's notice—several times a day. They were educated hunches each time though, keeping up with his research, so Kelly just let him hunch away.

She sniffed the air. It smelled like the right lead. "Okay. So any fakelore around hangings? Something to do with lynchings? Sorry to take it there, but we still don't know what we're dealing with."

"I'll do the research. And now, I have to ask. What makes you think this second kid is dead and not dormant like Tonya was?"

Kelly closed her eyes. It wasn't the psychic scent. It was more subtle than that. Claircognizance—she just knew it. Knew it in her bones and in her guts and in her womb. His neck wasn't cleanly severed like Tonya's. It was crushed. There was nothing clean about it.

"Trust my hunch, Critter? I trust yours. You're the data and research guy. I'm the psychic."

Critter stuck out his lower lip. "Fair. I'll trust you. But what if—"

"If he's not dead, we'll figure that out as we go. But between his broken neck and his crushed windpipe, I have no idea how to 'coagulate' him. And before you bring it up, we are not going to fuck around trying to make zombies. Resurrection is the business of gods, and I don't fuck with that. Now please go take that sample to your pink-hair friend and let me do some intuiting."

Critter made a stank face and said, "Yes ma'am."

When he'd left the office, Kelly opened the wonder closet and pulled out her Dreamachine. She could've made one of her own—it was simple enough to craft—but this one had supposedly belonged to William Burroughs himself. She bought it off the hexweb, even without giving it a psychic read. Luckily, the dreaming machine worked every time.

She lowered the plastic window shades in her office, rolled out a yoga mat she never once used for yoga, plugged the machine into the wall, and lay down beside it.

The light inside the cylinder blinked on as the turntable began to spin at 45 rpm. Through the yodh-shaped cutouts, sprays of light swirled around the room, flashing past her eyes. She closed them and let the light pulse against her eyelids, concentrating on feeling the little fluctuations of her pupils as they responded to the pulsing light. She soon entered the hypnagogic state.

On the shore between waking and dreaming, she saw images like the ones Tonya had described yesterday. She was in fog or cloudy water, and globes of light floated around her. She saw Tonya's body fall apart and come together and then fall apart again. When the parts came together, it smelled like sex. When they came apart, it smelled like birth.

From a limb grew limbs: Tonya's left arm grew out into a tree, rich brown bark and lush emerald leaves, and from the branches dropped teenage drifters, hanged from ropes like the newest victim. These ropes were visible.

Under this tree, Kelly saw women, naked and curvy, weaving rope. Their faces were like Olmec statues, and their skin shone like red clay in the light of the moons. She looked up to see the hanged kids gone, just Spanish moss left swaying in the breeze. She looked back to the weaving women, and they all stopped and stared at her.

Then the scream. Kelly heard an ear-piercing shriek and felt the weight of her consciousness slam back into her body. She sat up so fast she hurt her neck, and her heart pounded like a pestle in a mortar. When she caught her breath and calmed herself, she switched the Dreamachine off and yanked the plug from the wall. She put it back into the wonder closet with her other occult paraphernalia and slammed the door.

The Garuda car dropped her off at her building an hour later. This driver was chatty. She tried her best to be polite when she told him twice it wasn't a good day for her to talk. The man twice asked her if she was "sure she didn't want to talk" and said, "Penny for your thoughts? Sometimes a good talk is all that's needed. Just my two cents!" Kelly couldn't tell if he was hitting on her or just generally ignoring her boundaries—either way, fuck this guy. Not today, Garuda.

Kelly slipped a little of the hot foot powder under the driver's seat before she got out. She had no idea what that would do in the interior of a car. Maybe he'd sell it. She hoped he'd feel restless and unfulfilled for a good long while. Prick.

She waved at him as she used the app to tip him a single cent. *Penny for my thoughts,* she wrote in the review. Damn, it felt good to charge this to Sophia Martinetti.

The rickety elevator took her to the third floor of the old apartment building. Lots of older Seattle places didn't even have an elevator, built as they were for the World's Fair—way before ADA codes. Living on the third floor and doing her laundry in communal basement machines without an elevator would be its own special kind of urban hell.

The elevator dinged, and she heard the neighbor children shouting as she walked down the hallway. The mirrors and charms on her door rattled when she opened it, and the hamsa fell from its hook. She steadied herself with her cane as she crouched to pick up the protective hand-shaped charm. The glass eye on it had cracked. Kelly grumbled and hoped it wasn't an omen.

She used her tiny bathroom and brewed some coffee in her tiny kitchen. The building had been fine when she'd moved in. Good enough was good enough. The large bedroom was decent compensation for the shitty bathroom and kitchen, plus it had a brand-new washer and dryer in the unit. No basement pantie raids for her undies. The southern exposure was great until they cut the trees down. Lately, fourteen hundred a month to live here really bugged her, and the building deteriorated faster than she could lower her standards. When a kitchen cabinet door came right off in her hand and nearly broke her toes, she started budgeting to move.

Please let Martinetti fill my pockets with money, she prayed silently into her coffee. For all the charms and spells she knew, none of them ever made her rich. That didn't stop her from trying. Magic was unpredictable at best. It was a craft, not a science, and as far as crafts went, it was more like cooking than carpentry. Nothing tidy about it. Spells failed routinely, collapsing like a souffle. Other times, they had unexpected results. She'd try to manifest a new lover but end up missing her period for three months, despite no sex for the previous year.

It seemed to depend on the conjurer. Kelly had no talent for love or money spells, but she could smell evil from miles away. Maybe Sophia would teach her a spell for making serious bank.

Her phone buzzed with a text from Critter. *You okay? Came back and you'd locked up.*

She leaned against the counter for support and texted back, coffee in the other hand. *Knocked off way early. Bad trip on the dreamachine. Saw some stuff that made me think of Maya or Olmec magic. Find anything new?*

He didn't respond immediately. Kelly made her way over to her couch. Through the sliding glass door to the balcony, she watched hummingbirds joust by the red feeder. She wondered if they were male or female or if that even mattered to them in their turf wars over sugar water.

Critter's text came in: *Now I did. How's your neck?*

Kelly stopped breathing for a moment. She texted back: *How did you know I hurt my neck?*

Critter came right over and brought her a CBD edible. "You want some vapor too?" he asked, pulling out his v-wand.

"I mean, maybe? Yeah, yeah, I'll have some."

Soon they were both giggling, which hurt her neck, but she was too high to care by then. Her leg wasn't even tingling.

"Okay, okay, so . . . Ixtab." Critter got serious. "She's a Mayan goddess of suicide, usually by hanging. Ixtab is totally related to La Xtabay, who's a lot like La Llorona and La Malinche. They're all boogey-women like Medusa, who kill bad men and reckless children. And La Malinche can paralyze your neck. Lots of neck stuff happening. But here's the thing: there's, like, barely any surviving records of Mayan writing about Ixtab. The Spanish burned it all. The usual colonial atrocities."

Kelly stared at him, processing his ramble. "Uh huh. So the dangling kid. He was killed by Ixtab or Xtabay?"

Critter took a drag of vapor. "Oh, right. I'm not sure." He let out a cloud of cheap THC and continued. "Ixtab's not like that. She guides the suicides to Mayan heaven. She's a psychopomp and a goddess of mercy, but Xtabay is, like, the twisted postcolonial version of her. And she can paralyze your neck. Did I already say that?"

"Yeah."

"Oh, right. So guess what? The little we know about the original Ixtab may not even be authentic. She might be mostly mistranslation or made up by imaginative conquistadors."

"So she's also fakelore like Ti Kitha Demembre?"

He took a drag on the vapor wand. "Bingo. I don't think we're really looking for Vodou at all."

Kelly took the wand from him and cashed it. "We're looking for goddesses of misinformation. Well, shit." The cloud she exhaled curled around her head like a noose and dissipated.

By 4:30, the sun had set, and Critter was passed out on Kelly's couch. She was more stimulated than couch-locked by the drugs; the CBD hadn't counteracted the THC in the vapor as much as she'd expected, and she was no lightweight. She was body high but feeling very acute.

She spread a sheet of poster paper on her table and wrote *Goddess of Lies* across the top edge. She began to associate, spreading a web of words around the white void:

Misinformation Moon card 18 Serpent/fruit

Lies Hecate Lilith/fruit
Illusion Selene Apate
Laverna/Aradia Mistranslation Fall from Grace into Chaos
Fakelore Internet Colonized
Misinformation Kitsune Blamed for everything
Come Apollo in Bridal Dress, Shepherdess, Pythoness
Loki as mare, mother of Sleipnir
Jorogumo Mormo Tiamat
Horsefucker Loki
Meme Rumor Eris/Discordia/Apple

She ran out of ideas, so she pored over the list to see what further associations she could make. Were they jumping to conclusions? What if it wasn't just goddesses? What if fakelore and deceit weren't synonymous in this case?

The Loki reference stirred something but nothing clear or even powerful, like the way she knew the hanged boy was dead. Maybe they should take a day trip to Enumclaw to investigate the horse line of thought. No, that smelled entirely wrong.

Critter's phone buzzed so loudly it woke him up. He picked it up and handed it to Kelly and then put a throw pillow over his head. The message was from Harriet: *What the fuck did you bring me?*

Kelly raised an eyebrow and looked at Critter. She knew his phone passcode. *What did I tell you?* she wrote back.

You didn't. You just said not to tell anyone what I found when I tested it.

"Good boy," Kelly said aloud, and Critter just groaned. Kelly texted, *Should I come to you? I'll have to bring my cousin. She's the boss.*

She erased "boss" and tried to think of a better word. Was she the boss? Yeah. She was the boss. She typed it back in and sent the message.

After a quick shower, a massive dose of CBD, and a coffee, Critter was ready to go. His eye makeup had gone all smeary from the shower, and he was still wiping it away with a disposable cloth when the Garuda car came to take them both to the university's satellite lab.

"Should we be inconspicuous?" Kelly asked, gazing out the car window at the cityscape from I-5. The tingle in her leg came and went as the vapor high wore off.

Critter snorted. "Like we were 'inconspicuous' at the morgue? Nah. This isn't some high-tech, private biochem corporation we're visiting. It's fucking U of W. I doubt they even have security guards at this lab. They'll have some roaming around campus though. Just look like you're a hungry grad student who's supposed to be there."

"Done and done," she said. The driver didn't seem to be listening.

As Critter had expected, they waltzed right into the building, took the elevator to the fourth floor, and found Harriet's lab.

It wasn't as dark as Kelly had imagined—no cool neon lights in a tenebrous space—but it also wasn't bright. The ugly, yellowed florescent lights cast a jaundice over everything, and one of them flickered every now and then with a *tink-tink-tink*. Harriet wasn't even in a lab coat, just a black T-shirt. Haida formline tattoos in the shape of DNA helices curled around her arms.

The curious part was the smell, or lack thereof. It smelled like science, like sterile environments, but not like magic. Kelly expected the room to stink of magic as Harriet examined the stuff left behind when Tonya's arm evaporated.

"Okay, so, yeah . . . this is some weird, weird shit," Harriet told them. She let them look through the microscope at it, and Kelly didn't notice anything recognizable. Just a bunch of flotsam.

"Did you map the DNA?" Critter asked.

Harriet raised an eyebrow. "No. Firstly, do you know how long that would take? You can't just scrape something off your shoe and stick it into the Acme Magical DNA Machine. Besides, I'm not sure there is any DNA or RNA to work with. The sample *looks* like it came from something organic, but then there's other stuff I can't explain. There are no living cells—no nuclei, nothing I recognize."

She looked into the eyepiece again. "But it's arranged in the form of cells. There's something like cell walls but no stuff inside. It's not like animal or plant or fungal tissue, and it's not a batch of microorganisms clinging together. There's no sign of burning or melting, just goop made of empty cells. Is this some kind of nanotech shit?"

Kelly understood a little better. The sample illuminated in the microscope looked sufficiently organic to her untrained eye. Not the way she'd expect crystals to look, nor something neatly manufactured. She'd seen enough tardigrade YouTube videos to tell that this was at least supposed to look like it came out of a living thing. Now the question was: in that brief time that Tonya's lost arm manifested, was it alive, or was it something even stranger?

"I hope to gods it's not nanotech. I'm not prepared for that," Kelly told them.

Critter's self-control cracked. "We think it's magic."

Kelly glared at him. Harriet said, "Oh, well that makes more sense then. It's an illusion that closely resembles life but not entirely. It's probably just a bunch of ectoplasm. Don't quote me on that—as I've never seen ectoplasm under a microscope. It's pretty rare, but I guess you knew that. How the hell did you isolate ectoplasm anyway? I'm not an expert on spirits, just living things." Harriet smiled and brushed her baby pink hair out of her face. The dye was fading, and the bleach blond was starting to show through underneath.

Critter got more excited. "Ectoplasm! That is so *cool*! I mean, I should've guessed, but we collected the sample from—"

Kelly clapped her hand over his mouth, and his eyes said, *Fuck off.*

"That's enough out of you. Remember what we're dealing with here." She turned back to Harriet and asked, "What about living magic?"

"Huh?"

"You said you're not an expert on magic, just living things. What about living magic?"

Harriet pursed her lips. She looked back into the microscope and back at Kelly. "What do you mean? Like golems? Homunculi?"

Homunculi. There was a curious possibility. It smelled kind of right but not quite accurate. Tonya was a human being—flesh from flesh and blood from blood—and so was the hanged boy. Kelly was sure of that. The idea of replacing amputated limbs with lab-grown homunculus parts wasn't new, but Kelly had never heard of something this advanced. Other than the clean cuts of magical separation on her body, Tonya's arm cohered with the rest of her form seamlessly. If not the same arm she was born with, it had been a flawless copy. To the naked eye at least.

"It could be something like that. What about taking it to your other lab?" Critter asked.

Harriet grit her teeth. "I don't think that would be a good idea."

"Why not?" Kelly asked, picking up Harriet's ominous subtext.

"Because I'm new there, and they're very strict about who and what comes in and out, and security is tight, tight, tight."

"Jeez, what kind of private biotech are they working on?" Critter was rarely subtle.

"Stop asking questions about the other lab, or I'll have security remove you," Harriet told them.

Kelly would be following up on that mystery ASAP. "Okay, back to the stuff. It came from an organic source. We're not quite sure whether it was alive or dead when we obtained the sample."

Harriet scoffed. "Hope nobody died over this."

Kelly and Critter looked away.

"Oh shit. You're investigating a murder. Well, never done that before."

Harriet made a face like she was deciding whether to eat something from the back of the fridge, and then she said, "It's like I said, the sample is neither alive nor dead. It's something weird. Capital-W weird. It can't be cellular material because it lacks what living things require. But it was . . . I don't know . . . engineered? To look organic. Again, never seen ectoplasm or whatever this is under a microscope. Will you tell me more about the source? Did it come from, like, a ghost? Or a demon?"

Kelly had never seen nor smelled either, and she hoped she never would. "Not exactly, but something supernatural like that. Maybe preternatural."

Harriet's eyes brightened. "A zombie? I have never gotten my hands on a real live undead actual zombie."

"We're not sure what it was," Kelly said.

Critter chimed in, "Can you talk to some of your tribal elders about magic? Get some insights?"

Harriet blinked at him. "I mean"—she drew out the *N*—"I *could*. But I doubt any of my 'tribal elders' know dick from beans about alchemy. That's what we're talking about, right? The scientific method applied to the impossible? We don't really do that. If you want a soul recovery, I can hook you up, but we're not witch doctors. You're more likely to find a white girl shaman in Seattle than an indigenous one."

Kelly stifled a laugh. Critter gritted his teeth in embarrassment. "I'm sorry. Was that insensitive?"

Harriet laughed with her whole body. "Fuck sensitivity. How thin do you think my skin is?"

Critter apologized again. Harriet said, "If there's nothing else, I need to get back to work. I've told you everything I know about this sample. Keep me posted if it's not too top secret. Oh, and did you bring me anything to exchange?"

Critter pulled a protection amulet out of his pocket. "I made this for you. For clarity and protection."

Harriet took it and held it to the light. It was a chunk of quartz wrapped in a leather band. "I love it, Critter. ʔutʼigʷicid čəɬ." The last part sounded to Kelly like, "Oo-oot ig-weet-zee cha-tkh."

"Just curious. What does that mean?"

Harriet smiled. "It's 'we thank you' in Lushootseed. The language of my tribe. Just don't ask me to spell it."

In the elevator, Kelly berated Critter. "Why do you insist on revealing unnecessary information from our biggest case ever to brand-new contacts? This is serious, Critter. Organized-crime serious. Industrial-espionage serious. People are literally dying over this mystery drug."

Critter put up his open hands in surrender. "Dude, I'm sorry, okay? Harriet's trustworthy. And would we have gotten the ectoplasm data if we hadn't given her more context to work with? I saw your brain kick into high gear when she mentioned homunculi and golems."

The elevator didn't even ding, just came to rest on the ground floor and opened. They walked the empty hallway to the same door they'd entered, the tap of Kelly's cane making a soft echo down the passage. Kelly was so incensed with Critter that she didn't realize that her leg wasn't tingling.

Outside, they waited for the Garuda car in the dark.

"Miss? Miss, can you help me with a dollar or two for the bus?"

Kelly and Critter turned to see a bare-chested man with disheveled hair, standing a few feet away. Something about him was off but not in a way she recognized at a glance. He didn't seem to be ill, and he moved too gracefully to be intoxicated. Something about him was just too put-together for a half-naked man who begged college students for bus fare.

"Um, sure, I have two bucks," Kelly said and swung her purse to the front of her body. That's when she smelled it. Not body odor—in fact, she couldn't smell the man at all. It was the filthy, velvet smell of something demonic, a smell of wine and gold and innocents burned alive.

Critter blurted, "Jesus fuck!" and yanked her back. The man had turned away from them, and his back was alive. With only a trickle of blood, a series of quills or thorns sprouted, followed by a dozen of his vertebrae. They pulled themselves out of his flesh on their crablike legs, and their exit made wet, sucking sounds, leaving a red furrow where the middle of the man's spine had been. Through rictus or diabolism, his torso was still upright.

"Run!" Critter bolted, forgetting in his panic how difficult it was for Kelly to move quickly. The demon scent had primed her adrenaline, and she planted her feet and swung her cane as hard as she could at the man's neck. She got him between the shoulders, and he went down.

The bone crabs did not. They scurried toward her, too many for her to smash them all. She tried though, fighting her instinct to recoil and instead going down to her knees and either bashing them into the ground or knocking the infernal things across the grass like croquet balls. She got four or five of them before they were on her.

Their psychic scent was worse than anything she'd ever smelled—like pure hell itself, lakes of vomit and shit set aflame and a lot of blood. She felt some of them break the skin, either with their teeth or those spiny yellow crab legs or gods knew what appendages. Kelly tried to remain calm and find some way to repel them.

"Fuck you, demons!" Critter screamed, back in the nick of time. He ripped open his packet of hot foot powder and sprinkled it all over her. The things vibrated and started scrambling in all directions.

"Stay still! Stay still!" Critter shouted, though every nerve in her body told her to get as far away as she could. She tried to get up, but he held her down.

"It's just instinct and hot foot, Kelly. Breathe. You have to stay down to stay safe."

She started crying in frustration and fear, but she kept it together enough to pull a saltshaker out of her purse and shove it into Critter's chest. He took it, cranked the cap off with his teeth, and sprinkled it in a tight circle around them. That would hold for now and buy them time to think.

The man, if it was a man, was up again, swaying in grotesque arcs without his spine for support. He circled them but didn't get too close. His vertebral crabs skittered up and down his body, maybe unable to burrow back into his spinal column as long as the hot foot was working. He picked up some of the smashed ones and threw them at Kelly, but they lost momentum and dropped outside of the salt circle.

Critter held Kelly tightly while she calmed her mind and body and told her muscles to stay put.

"What the hell is he?"

Kelly's sobs became softer. "I was going to ask you."

The bone crab man still circled, mumbling things she couldn't make out, if they were even an earthly language.

"I've never read about anything like this. Do you think it's connected to bardo?"

Kelly let out a short peal of laughter. "Oh, *ya think*? Jesus, Critter. It doesn't take a psychic."

In a catlike motion, Critter swept up one of the smashed bone crabs and brought it into the circle. It twitched a little, but it neither attacked nor fled. Critter bound it up with red yarn to render it harmless and tucked it into his messenger bag.

The bone crab man startled and lunged toward their right. It was Harriet, running at them and brandishing a tree branch. She and the bone crab man ran at each other, and Harriet screamed something in Lushootseed. As the man got close, she whacked him with the tree branch, and he exploded into the little bloody bone crabs. They burrowed into the earth as Harriet stomped and whacked the stick against the ground and screamed more banishing spells in the tongue of her grandmothers' grandmothers.

"Holy shit, Harriet!" Critter said. "That was awesome! You saved our lives!"

Harriet walked up to the salt circle, and as soon as Critter stepped out of it, she slapped him so hard he fell to the ground.

"What the fuck did you drag me into, Critter? You're fucking lucky I had the thuja branch. Did you see that thing? That was a fucking demon, Critter. A demon!" She turned her head away and spat. "Fuck!"

The salt circle counteracted the power of the hot foot dust by then, and Kelly got up. "I am so sorry, Harriet. I have no idea why we were attacked. I mean, I kind of do, but no one warned me that something remotely like this could happen." A quick lie to deescalate the situation. Martinetti had been very clear about the possibility of monsters.

Harriet sighed and looked around in frustration. "Yeah, fine. You owe me dinner and an explanation." She used the thuja leaves to dust as much of the powder off Kelly as she could. "You don't happen to have some sage or a wing fan on you, do you?"

Kelly shook her head. Harriet grumbled, "Just what I want to do on a Friday night—fight fucking demons."

"I knew we were getting into some serious shit, but this . . ." Kelly stared at her plate. They all got fried chicken and waffles at the Lost Lake Café and comfort-ate until they all calmed down.

The server had asked what happened to them when he saw them at their table, and Harriet just said, "Demons. I'll have a sweet tea please."

"Do we know it was a demon?" Critter was glued to his phone, looking up everything he could think of to find anything on bone demons and magical vertebrae. "I'm not finding anything in the usual places."

"So don't look in the usual places," Kelly told him. Critter was still likely to blab anything and everything to Harriet, so Kelly cast a cloaking spell around their booth (after the food had come, of course). No one would notice what they talked about and probably wouldn't even remember they'd been there.

She let Harriet know as much as she felt she owed her but nothing more. "A private client hired us to gather some information. That led us to . . . a comatose victim with a severed limb. That stuff came off the severed limb."

Harriet cleaned the meat off a chicken bone and said, "How the hell did you get ahold of a severed limb? I'd think if it couldn't be reattached, it'd be incinerated."

"That's classified," Critter said, suddenly putting on professional airs. Kelly and Harriet both rolled their eyes.

"And the demon?" Harriet asked. "What was that all about?"

Kelly sipped her diet pop. "I honestly don't know. I never would've knowingly put you in danger like that. The client warned us we would encounter monsters if we got too deep, but I hadn't expected them to show up so soon. Or to track us down."

"Look, Kelly. I'm a scientist. Not a witch. I know some herbs and folk cures, but I am way out of my depth here. I don't want to be part of it. Besides, aren't monsters your specialty, Critter?"

Critter coughed. "Academically? Yes. Romantically? Hell yes. But the ones

I've dated—even the gumiho—never actually tried to kill me, or whatever that guy was trying to do. I have never seen nor heard nor read about anything like that. Spinal crabs are slapping new to me."

Harriet dragged the side of her fork against her plate, pushing the excess syrup around but not eating it. The three were silent for a while until Harriet said, "Who's good at divination?"

"Kelly is. Real good. Why?" Critter watched Harriet make little designs in her syrup.

"Because I'm not, but I'm seeing some crazy shit on this plate."

It wasn't from tarot or the *I Ching*, not even tea leaves or bird flight, but a talented oracle could sync to anything and make it talk. Chicken bones were common and good in a pinch, but she'd never tried it with maple syrup. Kelly switched sides of the table, sitting next to Harriet and gazing into the syrup and chicken bones. Harriet smelled good. She smelled like electricity and warm quilts, like intellect mixed with empathy.

"What do you see, Harriet?"

"I swear to god I see people hanged from trees."

Critter and Harriet both noticed Kelly stiffen. She couldn't see what Harriet could, but that wasn't necessary.

"Spit on the plate."

Harriet cocked an eyebrow, shrugged, and hawked up a wad of phlegm.

The second it hit the plate, Kelly saw spiders. Spiders and goats. She tilted the plate and watched the syrup and spit ooze around. There were horns and udders, hooves and palps, and too many eyes. Some were dark insect clusters, others had the long rectangular pupils of a goat.

"Well, that's fucked," Kelly said.

"What is? What do you see?" Critter swung his head like a dog, trying to see things from as many angles as possible.

"I don't see the same thing as Harriet. I see more creepy crawly things, but also goats. I don't think the spider things I see are the same as the crab things that came out of the demon's back."

Spiders and goats weren't bad omens, but they certainly didn't fill her with ease.

Harriet pushed the plate away and said, "If I die, I'm going to haunt you two forever. Like some Japanese *Ringu* shit, I swear to god."

☿

The car dropped Harriet back at the university lab where her brothers were already waiting. They carried more thuja and medicine for banishing evil spirits. The men glared at Kelly with wrath in their eyes.

The car pulled away. The driver didn't talk, and Kelly thought she might not speak much English. Kelly's leg blazed with her neuropathy, so at least the driver wasn't another monster. Just a lady trying to make ends meet.

"When's the last time you talked to your goddess?" Critter's question surprised Kelly but didn't rattle her.

"Oh, I don't know. I'm out of the habit, I guess. Been relying on my own power instead of something outside of me."

Critter bit his lower lip. "Lost your faith?"

Kelly laughed at that. "No, just misplaced it. Not using it."

"Is that good for your recovery?"

Kelly stopped laughing. She rolled her answer around in her head to make sure she believed it. She wasn't sure, but she said it anyway. "I'm never going back to using. I can't. I'll die. I want to live."

Critter put a hand on her knee. "I want you to live too. And with what just went down with Mister Crabby? I think it's time you called on your goddess for protection and strength."

She thought it over silently. *I suck at this. I'm the worst.* She was using every esoteric tool she had *except* for the one that used to matter most. When was the last time she'd prayed to Her?

Critter drummed his gold-lacquered nails on his knee for a while and then rooted around in his bag. "Um. Kelly?"

"Hmm?" She had started to doze.

"The crab is gone. The one I grabbed to study."

Kelly went on high alert. "Is it in here? Loose in the car?"

The driver immediately said, "I don't want no trouble. Did you bring an animal in here?"

Critter covered for them. "No, sorry to scare you. We're science students at the lab. We had a specimen in my bag, but it appears to have disintegrated."

"Disintegrated? I don't know this word," the driver said.

"Oh, it, um, melted. In my bag. It's harmless. Your backseat is still squeaky clean."

The driver let out a *humph* and kept eyeing them in the rearview. Kelly spoke quietly. "It melted? What the actual fuck?"

Critter opened his bag and showed her. There were some notebooks, pens, and makeup, but no demon crab. Instead, there was more black goo like the stuff left behind when Tonya's arm wilted away.

They didn't talk for a while. The city lights glistened in the rain on the window. Kelly stared past the human skyline and tried to make out the mountains beyond. Finally, Kelly's phone lit up. It was from Critter, silently discussing the case beside her. *I think we both know who you need to talk to.*

She looked at him and grimaced but texted back. *Who? A priest?*

Critter's expression didn't change, but he texted, *LOL no, sillypants. Who do you know that is intimately familiar with the drug trade?*

Kelly didn't even look at him. *Don't you dare,* she texted, her eyes blazing.

Oh fuck off. I'll say whatever I want. We're in over our heads, and I think it's time you consulted your ex.

The car pulled up at Kelly's building. She tipped the driver on the app before the car had even stopped. They both thanked the driver profusely, apologized for the trouble, and started bickering immediately when she drove off.

"Over my dead body, Christopher." She marched up the steps, stabbing the stone with her cane. Her leg was tingling like fire since they left UW.

"Considering that a demon just tried to murder us? I think it's a little late for 'over my dead body.'"

"I hate him, Critter. He ruined me."

"No, Kelly, *you* ruined you." Critters words made Kelly furious, but she also knew he was right. Critter went on, knowing his words weren't welcome but that Kelly would listen to him anyway. "He just helped you do it. And you've been un-ruining yourself beautifully for years."

Critter put his arm around her, a brotherly gesture that was suddenly awkward. "We need him, Kel. I know you can face him. It just means facing yourself."

Kelly let out a cynical chuckle. "Maybe he'll get killed by crab demons."

"We should be so lucky. I'll spend the night at your place for protection."

She turned to her cousin. "You think I can protect you from whatever this is?"

Critter frowned. "I meant I would protect *you.*"

A THOUSAND EGGS

"I'M DONE," SHE TOLD MARTINETTI ON THE PHONE.

"What do you mean 'you're done'? Things already getting too hairy for you?"

"A demon tried to kill me and Christopher. We don't even know what kind of demon it was."

"Huh. Weird," Martinetti said. The understatement rankled Kelly. "Did you two kill it? Can a demon even be killed?"

Kelly explained what happened without revealing what she learned from the maple syrup divination. She told Sophia every detail she could remember about the spine crabs as well as some of her speculation about the strange sample from Tonya's arm. Martinetti surprised her with some insights of her own.

"Yes, Harriet told me you'd been there. Surprise. Where did you think her other secret lab gig was? She's a great intern. Real potential in that one."

Of course, she worked for Martinetti. The connections and patterns were showing up more frequently. From a magical perspective, everything in the universe connected: matter, energy, ideas. The trick was to find a connecting thread or node or ley line and follow it to the desired effect. These threads practically sizzled, much more than the usual esoteric leads, and Kelly had started to wonder if she was at the center of something huge. That would imply a few things she wasn't ready to accept yet.

"And the demon sample also melted in Critter's bag? Hmm. It does sound like ectoplasm to me. Did you save any of it?"

Kelly sighed emphatically into the phone. "You aren't listening to me."

"I assure you I am. And I did tell you there'd be monsters. Well, for what it's worth, I'm sorry for the trouble. You're doing great work, and I don't want you getting attacked for it. I'll create a smoke screen for you. An extra cloak to take the heat off, divert attention. I assume you're already cloaking yourself, right?"

This bitch.

"I said I'm done." Kelly overenunciated the words. "Complete sentence. *I am done.*"

She heard Martinetti draw a lungful from a cigarette and the tiny plosive as she removed it from her lips. She drew out the exhale, letting Kelly know in doing so that her next words would be as weighty as Kelly's.

"Okay, so you're done. Now you listen to me. I'm sorry that you're on the demonic radar now. I'd hoped it would take another week at least before anyone noticed you investigating. But you *are* on their radar. At this point, you're safer under my protection than you are quitting. We're playing a dangerous game here, and our opponent is a pro. Let me take care of you, so you can do your best work."

Martinetti had her—as Martinetti had planned it. Kelly walked right into it. All for money. She went on, as she always did.

"You want me to sweeten the pot? I'll pay you a flat fee. Half a million instead of your hourly. You could buy a house."

It was a bit of an insult, though probably not intentional, like Martinetti's usual backhanded comments.

Kelly grumbled. "What good is a house if I'm dead? Do I haunt it?"

"Let me finish. I'll provide you with protection. I'll send Aweke over right now. Try to get some sleep, will you?"

Saturday, January 4

The call from Aweke came at about three in the morning. Kelly had changed her mind twice before leaving the ringer on overnight.

"Got another body. How soon can you be on Cap Hill?"

Kelly squinted and smacked her lips, trying to get her brain clear. "It's three. We were attacked by a spine-crab-demon-thing a few hours ago. Why aren't you here like Martinetti said you'd be?"

"Change of plans. Sorry, not sorry. I'll send a patrol car to pick you up."

Kelly groaned and looked over at Critter. He was snoring.

"Are you absolutely sure this is a bardo death?"

There was some commotion on Aweke's side of the call. He yelled something away from the receiver and then told Kelly, "Did you say crab demon? That's new to me. I need you to fill me in when you get here. And if this isn't bardo, then we have some heavy bioweapon shit to deal with. Just get down to Steampipe on Union. You know where that is? It's kinda tucked away."

Kelly didn't know the place, but she assumed Critter did. "I'll be right there. Get me a coffee, yeah?"

"Pfffff," Aweke razzed into the phone. "Get your own coffee, woman. But I don't think you'll want to be eating or drinking when you get in here."

It took Kelly a few attempts to wake Critter. Vapor was a pretty tame drug, but it might as well have been called "stupor" for how it affected Critter. He perked right up though when Kelly told him they were headed to Steampipe.

"Oh shit, I haven't been there in a while. I hope it wasn't anyone I know." He put the coffee maker on in Kelly's kitchen.

Kelly looked up what she could on her phone. Steampipe was a bathhouse in Capitol Hill, the local gayborhood and nightlife district. Plenty of folks fucking around with magic down there, but it was all kid's stuff, cantrips and sex magic. Occult homicide wasn't normal—anywhere—but if it were going to happen in Seattle, she wouldn't have guessed it would be there.

"Did Aweke say what the, erm, symptoms were this time?" Critter asked from the kitchen. Kelly heard him pour cereal into a bowl.

"Nope, just like last time. If it's another spontaneous dismemberment or an invisible noose, at least that gives us a pattern. If it's something else out of left field, that also helps me get a broader understanding of what's going on. Intentional randomness isn't random at all. Now eat quick. Aweke said we won't want to eat anything at the scene. I hope that doesn't mean it's absolutely horrible."

It was absolutely horrible.

The victim was a Filipino man, mid-forties, identified by some of the other patrons as Daniel Gomez. None of them claimed to know him well: aside from seeing him out and about and occasionally having sex with him, the general consensus was that Gomez was very private. Some suspected he had a wife and family in another city, maybe even local, but the police database confirmed that he was single. He was an accountant, upwardly mobile middle class, living alone in his condo just down the street. Aweke told Kelly that a detective unit was on its way to Gomez's place now.

Luckily, there were several witnesses, like the incident with Tonya at the Deep. Still no leads on the hanged kid in the warehouse. These folks had less and less in common the more of them turned up. They didn't live in the same cities (assuming the hanged kid was a drifter), and they had differing age groups and genders and different ethnicities. That suggested it wasn't a serial killer.

"So we know they aren't being targeted for murder," Aweke told her as they surveyed the gore.

"Actually, we don't know that." Kelly corrected him, much to the detective's surprise. "Randomness itself is a pattern. The less these victims have in common, the more likely they were selected. I think someone's conducting tests on different demographics."

The chlorine smell of the well-maintained bathhouse cut through the worst of the stench of death. It was tolerable, but Kelly could smell human insides. And goats. And spiders. Critter vomited as soon as he walked into this room, and a weary but resigned officer blocked off the mush puddle of coffee and cereal to keep it from contaminating any evidence.

The increasingly familiar scent of bardo was there as well, though Kelly still couldn't pin the psychic scent to anything she'd ever experienced.

"How close can I get to the body?" she asked, stepping toward the corpse before getting permission.

"About that close," Aweke told her, stopping her after a couple of steps with a hand on her shoulder.

"What's wrong with his eyes?"

"His eyes?"

"That's what I said, Aweke."

"I'll get a closer look," he told her, holding her back with a palm against her chest. If he touched her breast, she'd knock him into next Tuesday with her cane.

He approached the body, stepping gingerly around the tile rim of the hot tub. Gomez was slumped on the stairs, his lap and legs in the water, his abdomen distended until his body cavity burst open. Guts spilled into the hot tub, floating around amidst a strange black foam.

Aweke used a sterile dowel to lift each eyelid and return them to their half-closed death glare. "His eyes are all fucked up. How did you notice that from over there?"

"I was looking for it. So the pupils are rectangular, right? Horizontal? That's how it looks from here."

Aweke handed the dowel off to an evidence collector. "Yeah. Like . . ."

"A goat?"

Aweke looked to be lost in memory. "Yeah. Goat."

"His body changed. I'm sure, if you asked any of the other patrons, they'd tell you this man's eyes were as human as anyone else's when he entered the hot tub. It's the bardo that made them change."

"The hanged kid didn't change. The coroner's been over the body ten times."

"But Tonya changed. She grew back a limb she'd lost years ago. Then her body separated."

"And the shredded abdomen? Looks like something inside came out, not like someone cut their way in."

Kelly stared at the black foam drifting around with the flotsam of the dead man's entrails. "Has anyone checked the tub? Because if something came out of him, it might very well still be in there. It might even be . . . alive."

"Alive?!" Critter said, finally getting his composure back. "Wicked!"

Aweke sneered. "Mun, bring your pet dog to heel. He's only here because you said he was essential."

Critter's mouth fell open like an attic door, and he said, "Excuse me, Mister Aweke, but I do not appreciate being talked down to—"

Aweke rolled his eyes. "God damn, you are so white. Just try not to interfere, okay?"

Critter raised an index finger to further object, but Kelly lowered his hand gently and told him, "I need you out there, not in here. Don't be obvious but ask around with the regulars. Find out everything you can, rumor or truth, about Daniel Gomez. Will you do that for me?"

Critter made a tongue-pop noise and said, "Fine. What about goat stuff? Fakelore on goats?"

Kelly pursed her lips and grit her teeth. "Not yet. I want to sniff around the scene a little more before we start that."

With that, Critter left.

"He's getting on my nerves, Mun," Aweke said.

"Yeah, he does that. So do you. But he's the best researcher I've ever worked with, so please try to make room for him. I rely on Critter for a lot of my leads."

Aweke smirked with only one side of his mouth. "Were you two raised together?"

Kelly stared at the black foam. "Does it matter?"

"I guess not," the police detective said, turning back toward the water. "Now, you think there's something in there?" He gestured with a new dowel.

"I think it's a distinct possibility, though I'm not sure what. All of this has been unpredictable since the beginning."

Aweke took a step back. "Yeah. Well, I don't want to fuck around and find out. I'll get animal control in here."

Before he could call in the dog catcher, some of the foam cleared, enough to present a different material floating amidst the viscera.

"What's that?" Kelly pointed at a cluster of slick black orbs. They floated on the water like bubbles, but bubbles didn't have protrusions with membranes stretched among them like fins.

"Hell if I know," Aweke said. "Not sure I want to either."

Kelly inhaled deeply. The mix of scents made her gag, but she got some new impressions. "Mermaid purses."

"I'm sorry, again?" Aweke looked at her as though she spoke nonsense.

"Mermaid purses. Like shark eggs. These are clutches of eggs. I can smell something in them, not alive exactly but . . . growing. Smells like goats and spiders and something else. Not fish or anything else aquatic."

"Okay, then we definitely need animal control in here. And a biohazard team. And—"

A sound, somewhere between a pop and a crack, echoed in the room. A tiny splash followed—and more popping sounds. Eggs hatching.

The hot tub churned with alchemical life as grotesque little animals broke the surface. Kelly and Aweke watched in frozen horror as the things writhed toward the dead man's body, swarming it.

The hatchlings were chimerical; Kelly could tell that much. Something insectoid mixed with something mammalian. The room got warmer as they emerged from the tub.

"It's a nest!" Kelly shouted. "This whole room is a nest!"

"Oh, fuck! Fuck fuck fuck!" Aweke shouted, and Kelly saw that one of the little monsters was on him. It jumped onto her hip and stared at her. It was a perverse little thing, no bigger than a billiard ball and with too many spindly black legs. Its head was like a baby goat's but with too many eyes. Those eyes looked right at her, and the thing screamed and made a lunge toward her face.

She swatted it away with her cane. More of the things emerged from the black foam, most of them moving toward the corpse—now feasting on it.

"Run! Just fucking run!" Aweke said, grabbing her hand. They always told her to run as if the thought never occurred to her.

He pulled her into a hallway and practically dragged her as she hopped behind him. Realizing that she couldn't keep up, Aweke lifted her over his shoulder—remarkably strong for such a thin man. His shoulder mashed into her belly, jabbing into her bladder.

He finally set her down in a small labyrinth of wooden panels and partitions. When she caught her breath, she said, "Um, thanks."

Aweke still panted, leaning forward with his head down and hands on his knees. "Don't mention it."

Kelly texted Critter, hoping the signal would make it out of the building. *Tub was full of monster eggs. They hatched. I'm lost inside building. U make it out ok?*

Mercifully, he texted back. *Yeah, outside now. WTF? Should I come get u?*

NO do not enter. I'll find my way out. Tell cops bio weapon went off.

She texted Martinetti next. *Help. Aweke and I trapped in steampipe bathhouse. Baby monsters everwhere. Civilians and cops too.*

By then, Aweke had his breath. "Now what?"

Kelly shook her head incredulously. "You're the cop. I got nothing."

"Nothing? No tricks, no charms, no spells? Thought you were a witch."

"Who told you that? Martinetti? I'm an occult detective, not a witch. Witches have a religion. I just use their tools."

"You forget your ancestors," Aweke said and added something in Somali that sounded like, "Da-qin aw-liss."

"Oh, fuck right off. Did *you* forget that we're lost in a sex club infested with baby monsters?"

"How could I possibly forget," he said, leaning and placing a palm flat against a wooden partition.

Kelly laughed at him. When he asked why that was so funny, she informed him, "You're leaning on a glory hole."

He didn't comprehend at first. "Like in glass blowing?" Then he caught on, jumping back from the wooden makeshift wall as if it was a hot stove.

Aweke cautiously approached the lozenge-shaped hole in the partition. "Why is it oblong? Why not round?"

"Different heights," Kelly told him. Aweke rolled his eyes as if to say, *How did I not think of that?*

Instead, he asked, "How long do you think we have until those things make it to this part of the building?"

Some men wearing only towels ran past, shrieking. "Not long," Kelly said. But Detective Aweke's awkward interaction with the glory hole gave her an idea. "Hey, do you happen to have a hagstone on you? Or a sacred bead?"

"You mean like a xirsi?" He felt around in his suit pockets. "Hang on."

He pulled out a short strand of glossy amber beads tied off at the end.

"Well, that'll have to do," Kelly said. "If you want to live through this, cut that and give me some beads."

Aweke grimaced but complied. Kelly took the beads, found one big enough to gaze through, and held it up to the glory hole. Peering through the bead, she saw dark energy churning. Blacks and charcoal grays swirled with deep, dark violet. There was enough delineation between the shades that she could see the strands of each color sucked downward, like watching paint water curl down a drain. It was enough of a lead.

"We gotta move. We're heading down." She didn't wait for a response before stabbing her cane to the floor and shoving off toward a door that read, "Employees Only."

Aweke started after her. "Down? Doesn't sound like an escape route to me."

Kelly didn't even look back. "It's a natural energy sink down there. It's clearing out the bad shit." She was through the door. As she guessed, it was a staff stairwell, lit by a single red bulb in a safety cage on the wall. There was even a fire extinguisher, but she couldn't carry it and maneuver down the stairs at the same time.

Aweke jogged up and closed the distance between them, a step or two behind her on the stairs. "Kelly. Kelly! Remember where we are. This place is right on top of a major steam line. If we go much lower, we'll be in the steam tunnels, and I for one do not want to die boiled alive."

Kelly kept descending. "Do you want to die eaten by baby spider goats? Or giving traumatic birth to a thousand monster eggs? I don't."

One floor down, the stairs ended in another staff door. She pushed through, Aweke catching the door from behind her to hold it open. The smell hit her like a crow divebombing her face, and she felt faint for a moment. Aweke just ran the other way.

It was an office space lit garishly with fluorescent white ceiling panels. The contrast between this light and the spooky red stairwell would've been disorienting enough if not for the beast. A vile thing with too many limbs squatted in the middle of the room. It was hard to get a good look at it. At first, Kelly thought it was the sudden flood of artificial light messing with her eyes, but after staring aghast for a few seconds, she realized that the thing's body was partially liquid or gaseous.

The amorphous black lump of it would put out insectoid legs or feelers and retract others. It had a goat's head and neck with smaller goat heads budding like warts from the elongated throat. From several slits in the body, more black egg sacs oozed slowly out, pooling around the abomination.

In an almost comedic moment, it cocked its head to the side and looked as shocked to see Kelly as she was to see it. Then it screamed.

The ambient music of the sex club changed to an egregious extended cut of Pepper Mashay's "Dive in the Pool." *Beep, boop, beep beep boop.*

Aweke came crashing down the stairs and through the doorway behind Kelly, wielding the fire extinguisher. He pulled the pin and emptied the canister into the hive queen's face. *Beep, boop, beep beep boop.*

The mix of propellant and powder fogged out the room. The creature screamed again. Pepper Mashay screamed on the PA system. And Aweke screamed like a warrior howling at the enemy on the battlefield.

Beep, boop, beep beep boop.

Before the fog swallowed it up, Kelly made a quick assessment of the only other door, the one on the far side of the room that said "Caution: Hot Pipes." She galloped over to it, curving wide to avoid the Goat Queen or whatever the fuck it was, and shouldered her way through.

Behind her, she heard Aweke shout something—probably the Somali equivalent of "fuck you!"—and then the sound of the extinguisher smashing against something organic. *Beep, boop, beep beep boop.*

A few moments later, Aweke stumbled into the machinery room to find her. It was hot in there, though not as hot nor humid as Kelly had expected. Here, steam heat from the city's pipe system was rerouted throughout the bathhouse, warming the building in winter and heating the water year-round. Kelly peered again through the amber bead and saw the swirling energies spiraling around her on their way down into the earth.

"I think we found the energy sink. Makes sense with all the flowing water vapor."

"Steam. Right. Fire plus water."

"Mmm-hmm. Cleansing. The thing in the next room won't follow us in here. I think we're safe at least, and we may even be able to use the steam tunnels to get out."

She felt a subtle tug as she said it, some energy thread pulling her toward the heart of the steam tunnel network. No, not the heart. The guts.

"Yeah, about that. We don't have protective gear. How are we going to avoid being boiled?"

She resisted the pull of energy. Julian was right—the guts of the city would literally digest them if they went too far in. She didn't know any spells or charms for shutting off a municipal heating system, neither city-wide nor precisely along the exit route they needed. That was some high-wizardry, way beyond what she and Critter could do, but magic worked in many forms. Money was one of them.

"Can you get Martinetti on the phone?"

Aweke looked at his cell. "No service."

"Not even wifi?"

He gritted his teeth. "Woman, do you think this sex club has public wifi? You got their password?"

They both looked at the door that separated them from the office and the abomination inside. Kelly cocked an eyebrow at Aweke.

"No. I am not going back in there," he swung his arms, crossing and uncrossing them manically.

"Fuck it. I'll go get it," Kelly said. She sidled up to the door and looked through the peeping window. "Um. Aweke? It's gone. What did you do to it?"

"What do you mean it's gone?" He shoved her out of his way and looked through. *This asshole,* she thought.

She pushed the door open, and Aweke fell on his face. Kelly limped into the room and scrutinized the space. On the floor was the empty extinguisher cannister, the butt end spattered with black sludge. From a pool of the brackish stuff, there trailed a rough, looping smear where the creature had dragged its bulk toward an exit, but then the stain just stopped. No body, no more eggs, nothing. She checked the ceiling—Critter had warned her that some monsters like to perch and strike from the ceiling—but no, the pressboard tiles were intact and clean.

"It's just gone?" the police detective asked. "Evaporated? Teleported?"

Kelly thought a moment. "Maybe *dissipated*. Or maybe it never really existed to begin with."

Aweke rubbed his bleeding lip on his sleeve. "It certainly existed when I beat its face in with the fire extinguisher."

"Do you have any evidence bags on you?"

He did, and he and Kelly found a roll of paper towels and mopped up some of the black residue and bagged it.

"When we put Tonya's body back together, her arm withered and dissipated, leaving some crud behind. That was the arm she lost as a kid, but somehow, it grew back when she OD'd on bardo. Critter bagged one of those crab demons, but it also dissolved into black goop. I bet you this crud is made of the same stuff."

"And what would that be, hmm? Moon dust? Fairy piss?"

"You're probably not far off. Let me know when your people analyze it. I'll do the same. Now, can you grab the wifi password and call Sophia?"

"This place is a mess. We could be looking for hours."

"It's literally posted on the wall next to you," Kelly informed him. It was one word, all lowercase: sendtopsnotcops.

He narrowed his eyes and then punched it into his phone. Kelly could only hear his side of the conversation, but that sufficed. "Yes. No. Yes, no, I know that. We need you to get us out. Well, Miss Mun thinks we should risk the steam tunnels, but if you can get us out the front door, I would prefer it. Yes, then send in the cleaners after. We're in the office in the basement."

Half an hour later, some folks in hazmat suits escorted the two of them out the front door as requested. Critter was watching from across the street, and he ran over and asked a thousand questions, one for each black egg laid by the Goat Queen.

☿

Dawn was breaking in one of Martinetti's offices by the time the four of them had settled. Kelly and Critter had about two and a half hours of sleep apiece, but encountering demonic beasts twice in one night was enough to keep them alert.

"Spidergoats and spinal crabs. We're certainly deep in the devil's asshole now, aren't we?" Martinetti flicked a cigarette ash into a coffee mug on her desk.

"Do you have to smoke right now?" Aweke asked.

Martinetti drew a puff and held it. "No." Then she exhaled slowly, acting like the head-bitch-in-charge she loved to be.

"Whatever," Aweke said. Kelly and Critter snickered at Martinetti's flex. She'd already ordered breakfast for them, and the two cousins wouldn't turn that down.

"We're on the clock, people. I'm not fond of staying up all night either. Talk to me. What do you think is going on?"

Aweke ran his palm over his close-cut hair and said, "Well, there could be many things at work here—"

Kelly brought her coffee cup down on the table with a bang and cut Aweke off. Martinetti smirked at that.

"It's not time for any of us to be coy," Kelly told the group. "I still want to wrap this case up and get the hell out before one of us gets killed. So here's what we've got: bardo seems to have some sort of tie to ectoplasm. Something illusory that looks and acts like living tissue for a while and then dissolves and leaves a residue. That's what Tonya Williams's mysterious missing-then-not-missing limb was made of before she came back to life and it evaporated."

"Ectoplasm. That's good," Martinetti said. "Hadn't thought of working with that before."

Kelly continued. "Maybe bardo is made of ectoplasm. Maybe it just produces ectoplasm. I don't know. What I do know is that the creature we encountered in the office of Steampipe smelled like bardo. And it disappeared, just like Tonya's arm. Just like the little bone crab thing that we bagged, though that smelled like a real demon. I don't know, magic is weird."

Martinetti put her beige Louboutins up on her desk, the red soles pointed at her. Kelly was glad Sophia wore a pantsuit today. "The goat with a thousand eggs. Where have I heard that before?"

In an instant, Critter whipped out his phone and searched. "The Goat of the Woods with a Thousand Young," he read. "It's Shub-Niggurath. Fictional fertility goddess-slash-demon-slash-alien. Lovecraft invented her. It. Them?"

Aweke looked impressed. Martinetti stared like stone.

"Shub-Niggurath even has a gaseous cloud form. I don't find anything about spiders—but goats definitely. And most fan art shows her with tentacles, but in some, she has pincers or insect legs."

"More fakelore then." Kelly got out her tablet and started making notes.

"Not exactly," Critter said, still scrolling through his phone. "Fakelore is word of mouth and urban legends and other concepts that enter the folklore conversation, even though none of it is part of the original lore. Ti Kitha Demembre is definitely fakelore, at least the divided goddess stuff. Ixtab is a gray area. She probably existed but was reinterpreted by colonizers. Shub-Niggurath—god I don't even like saying that name—she started as overt fiction and was turned into cult folklore by a bunch of nerds who wanted to be wizards."

"But either way, she's another fictionalized goddess. She fits the pattern to a T." Kelly sniffed for more but couldn't get any psychic information beyond the immediate and the obvious.

"This is all a bit of a stretch. Don't you think?" Aweke said. Martinetti stared at him with a mixture of detachment and irritation. He went on, "Well, don't you? A drug made of magic and ghost jizz, sold on the street to teenage hobos and club kids and middle-aged accountants, and that kills people by turning them into gods and goddesses that don't even exist? Magic that turns you into a story. It's absurd!"

Martinetti turned and stamped out her cigarette on the window behind her. "Everything is absurd, Julian. Money is absurd. Love is absurd. Religion and magic are particularly ludicrous, but they still exist, and they hold power. That's why I hired Kelly. And Critter. Can I call you Critter?"

Critter did his little inhale that Kelly knew meant a stream of redundant talk was coming, and she cut him off as readily as she did with Detective Aweke.

"The Occult Crimes Division is very new, and I don't think they get it," Kelly said. "Like putting white cops in Black and brown neighborhoods." Julian Aweke's eyebrows lifted at Kelly's words, but he kept listening. "They can take the notes and follow orders and do their best, but they'll never really get it. Same with applying traditional detective work to the occult."

Aweke shifted in his seat, clearly uncomfortable, not sure what to say. Martinetti laughed softly and batted her mink extension eyelashes. They weren't overbearing. They were expensive and tight and perfect. Kelly caught herself checking Sophia out. She was sexy as hell, Kelly had to admit. Too bad she was a rich jerk. Kelly could at least use the "never with a client" excuse.

Martinetti moved her legs down from the desk and sat up, rigid. "Okay, so we're not being coy, and we also shouldn't waste time trying to one-up each other."

"From you, of all people," Critter murmured, giving her side-eye as he sipped his coffee.

Martinetti looked at first like she might stab him in that eye, and then she cackled. "Okay, I like you. I didn't at first, but you've got guts. Feminine men always do."

"Still one-upping each other," Kelly said.

Aweke crossed his legs and frowned. "So what is the connection then—between bardo and these fakelore gods?"

"Goddesses," Critter insisted. "Shub-Niggurath is beyond gender, but Ti Kitha and Ixtab are feminine figures. That has to be significant. Kelly?"

The others stayed graciously silent while Kelly mulled it over. "Probably. I'll use some of my tools and see what kind of connections present themselves. The goddess versus god thing could be promising. I still come back to the fact that they're all recent creations. All reinterpretations or misinterpretations. The gender stuff seems secondary to that, but I don't know yet. Good leads either way."

Breakfast arrived, and the group continued comparing notes over benedicts and compote. Martinetti made notes on her tablet. When they'd all eaten their fill, their paymaster made a few emphatic stabs to the tablet screen and said, "Okay. Kelly and Julian, you're both getting bonuses for worker's comp. Sorry about all the weird shit that's been trying to kill you. Critter, I trust you and Kelly can work out your own bonus."

Critter swiveled his head from side to side and said, "Thanks?"

"And about the 'weird shit trying to kill you' part. Julian, you're now assigned to watch Kelly and Critter twenty-four-seven. Keep them—and yourself—locked down. I've arranged a safe house for you. It's triple cloaked. I'll be goddamned if any demon or half-cocked warlock can track you there. I can send you more muscle if you need it, but I doubt any of you want to work with the kind of people available to be bodyguards on short notice. Also, take this."

She handed Kelly a small, unlabeled canister that looked like an airhorn or a mini fire extinguisher. "I had the lab concoct it. That's psychic mace. Spray it at a spirit or a psychic or a warlock and it will fuck them right the fuck up. It has everything in it from sage to agua de florida. Also some real bear mace, so don't spray it at anyone you don't want to torture. You could take down a barghest with that stuff."

Aweke said, "What about my job? The precinct will notice I'm gone."

Martinetti flared her nostrils and said, "*This* is your job. I've taken care of it. There's an authority loop that will look like you're in deep cover with no supervisor. It'll take them at least a week to work that out at the OCD."

"OCD?" Critter asked.

"Occult Crimes Division," Kelly said. Critter should've figured that out by now.

"Oh! Ha! Who fucked that acronym up when they were naming the department?"

Martinetti grunted and said, "We're in the big leagues here. I haven't seen this kind of conjuring since Dr. Leng. I'm not sure who could be behind it. Leng is dead—thank god—and he never took on apprentices. Too stingy with his magic. The whole street drug angle isn't Charlotte Bamford's style, and Soames doesn't have the balls for this. Maria Dorn could pull off the chemistry—we need to get her on our payroll—but not the demon. My best guess at this point is it's some uppity warlock from outside the country."

Sophia tapped a perfect nail on her tablet screen. "Keep. Digging. I'll handle the Asian and European markets. They keep to themselves usually, but alchemy and hubris go hand in hand. I've considered tapping into the East Asian trade, but I don't want to spend eternity at the bottom of the Pacific. Let them have their turf."

Now she was just showing off. Aweke yawned.

Kelly convinced Critter and Aweke to make a pit stop at the Non-Linear Investigations office, so she could raid the wonder cabinet. She had the demon mace ready, but luckily, no monsters lurked there.

Once the three of them were secured in the safehouse, Kelly asked to be alone. The men grudgingly let her. She shut herself into a windowless bedroom.

Something Aweke said back at the bathhouse really rankled her. The thing about forgetting her ancestors. She hadn't forgotten anything. Her father didn't like to talk about life back in Korea. He told her that her grandparents were dead. She suspected that they were not.

She knew her mother's family back a few generations, but that knowledge ended at Ellis Island. She didn't want to find out more about who they were and what they fled from. Both her parents were Catholic, and the subject of witchcraft was forbidden. She was never allowed to be a ghost or a monster on Halloween, only princesses when she was little and then doctors and astronauts and other respectable professions when she was older.

She sat cross-legged on the floor and spread her assorted esoteric tools. Cards and bones and crystals. A little of this and a little of that, mostly American stuff—whether indigenous, diaspora, or appropriated culture. There was nothing of Muism there, no Taoist neidan, nothing to tie her to the Korean branch of her ancestry.

What are you avoiding? she wondered. Ben used to ask her that, and thinking about Ben made her think about Rattlesnake. Those were issues for another time, another ritual.

Kelly made herself relax. She concentrated on the goddesses. *Ixtab.* Three feminine spirits. *Ti Kitha Demembre.* Three inventions from fanciful imaginations—men's imaginations, no doubt. Three very different pantheons. *Shub-Niggurath.* Three spirits of violence and fertility.

She thought about the victims. They had nothing in common, not even the ways they died. Not all of them were even dead. *Every set has something in common,* she told herself. *Every human is connected to the next. I am tangential to every living thing.* She felt the subtle change in energy inside her and followed the lead.

She sank into herself, meditating on the koan of sameness and the not-sameness of every person on the planet. *I am everything. I am nothing. I do not end. I do not begin. I am a bubble. I am the sea.*

She could feel the smaller soul-self inside of her glowing—the essential Kelly Mun, unvarnished by ego or pain—shrinking and condensing until it landed in the lotus position behind her navel. Kelly breathed into this glowing core of herself, as little and full of life as a sesame seed. Self and not-self. The tea in the cup before and after the container shatters.

She imagined the threads of her attention and energy. A hundred crimson strings moored her to the distractions outside, and she concentrated on cutting them loose, one by one at first and then in twos and threes until they all fell limp around her. She pulled that attention back into herself and balled it up like yarn into her core.

She could feel that she was rocking now, her upper body swaying in the rhythm of the trance. She was present in her body, all her senses aware, thoughts brushed aside like a veil. Then she pushed out, projecting her astral form. Didn't even need her tools—she just left her body like it was a mat of bones.

She was in the Bardo—the real Bardo. It was just as Tonya had described it, like swimming through fog. For Kelly, it was more like dancing. She *was* the mist. To move was effortless.

The orbs of light drifted around her, and they were beautiful. The peace here was beautiful. Kelly felt utterly certain that she could die right now and go on in the Bardo with no attachments or regrets.

She heard chanting. 지장보살. 지장보살.

The words came to her more as vibrations through her form than as a sound in her ears. 지장보살. *Ji Jang Bosal.*

She smelled fresh, flowing water. A spirit coalesced their form in front of her. At first, she thought it was the young Christ, the one unknown during his adolescence, hidden from history. They looked so kind, like they could love a dead baby bird back to life.

Then she knew the spirit was Ji Jang—a bodhisattva of the dead, protector of children, guardian of the miscarried and stillborn, guiding them toward their next life on earth. They were water and light and mercy.

You have questions, Ji Jang said, their mouth unmoving. They didn't speak it in any earthly language. They sent it to her heart.

I don't know what to do, she told them. Her dark hair drifted around her face.

Yes. You do. Trust yourself, the genderless bodhisattva told her.

I don't even know what I'm looking for.

Yet you keep finding it. You found me, didn't you?

The spirit smiled and cupped their hands. Kelly moved closer. In the palms they held a fetus no larger than an apricot. It was fascinating, this tiny human thing.

I don't understand, Kelly said. She knew she wasn't moving her mouth either. There was nothing for sound to travel through, only intention.

There is no mystery here. This soul was due to be born. Their mother wasn't ready. Their mother sent them back to the Womb of Heaven. It is painful, but it simply is.

Did Ji Jang Bosal guide her here to the Bardo just to show her this? An abortion?

Is this the Womb of Heaven then?

The spirit laughed at that. The laughter was silent yet musical at the same time, like rain on windchimes.

The Cervix of Heaven perhaps. The gateway to the gateway. Ji Jang smiled. If she weren't completely in peace and wonder, Kelly might've thought the whole thing was ridiculous. She was drifting through a pocket dimension of the afterlife with the Buddha of dead babies, who was talking about a cervix. Of all the pantheons, the Buddhas were particularly light-hearted. Their sense of humor was quite literally legendary.

She concentrated on asking the most appropriate question. *How do I help the people that the bardo drug is harming?*

Ah, there's a question worthy of you. Ji Jang beckoned her to follow. Together, they reached a shore of smooth stones on the edge of a forest. They both stepped out of the mist.

Ji Jang sat on a patch of grass, and several children materialized around them, clinging to the spirit's robes. Kelly sat as well.

You need me to be enigmatic, so that is the form I take. I am no more mysterious than you require of me.

Kelly nodded, and a soul that looked like a toddler came over and sat in her lap.

She rephrased her question. *What do I do to help?*

Ji Jang brought their knees up and rested their chin on their crossed arms. *Those trapped in samsara don't often see a thing as it is. They only see things as they can recognize them. What you are calling bardo is not the Bardo. You know this. But people call it thus because they cannot conceive of what this new thing truly is.*

What is it, Ji Jang?

There are no words for it. It has no essence, yet it is essence. But you might compare it to condensed enlightenment, harvested from a pure source, beaten flat into a false dream.

Please, bodhisattva. You're still speaking in riddles.

No. I tell you the unblemished truth. I cannot make it any plainer. Find the source. Break the container. Free this new thing. I cannot do it for you because I belong here—with them.

More children emerged from the mist and from the forest. The one in Kelly's lap took her face in its tiny hands. *Are you my mother?* the little soul asked.

I'm sorry, little one. I am not, she told the child. The kid looked familiar, like she'd seen her in photographs long forgotten.

Oh. Maybe I'm your mother, ready to be born again.

Kelly stared into the child's face, and the instant of recognition brought her joy and confusion and pain all at once. It was her mother's face, as seen in the scant few childhood photos her mother kept.

Mama? Kelly engulfed the little soul in her arms, but the girl slipped through her arms like water. Ji Jang laid a hand on her arm.

I'll keep this soul safe. She is not your mother anymore. That cup is dust. Only the water remains. You must go now. Use what I've taught you.

She awoke choking on water. Aweke and Critter were there, lifting her to the air. The three of them were in a white, sober bathroom.

When she caught her breath, Kelly asked, "How the fuck did I get in the bathtub? With my clothes on?"

"You sleepwalked," Aweke told her. "You were in a trance."

"Yeah, Kel," Critter affirmed. "You got into the tub and turned the water on. We watched you but thought we probably shouldn't interfere unless you were definitely in danger. Were you?"

She breathed in the antiseptic air. The water was cold, and her heavy, sopping clothes clung to her skin.

"No. I think I was the safest I've been in days."

DR. BEN WEI

I**T HAD BEEN HER MOTHER'S DEATH THAT REIGNITED HER INTEREST IN THE** occult. At age twenty-five, too young to lose a mother to "natural causes," Kelly had watched as the chemo failed to shrink the cancer in her mother's brain. It only shrank her mother.

"Eyeballs and teeth," her mother had told her. "All I see when I look in the mirror is eyeballs and teeth." Mrs. Mun's hair had all but fallen out by then, leaving skeletal strands here and there atop her liver-spotted head . . .

It took months rather than years. It would've been weeks without the intervention of medicine. Her mother had the foggy thinking associated with chemo, but Kelly expected that: forgetfulness more than utter confusion. By the time Kelly went home for Christmas, her mother was in full dementia. She frequently refused food, water, and even medicine. She showered with her clothes on. The phone would ring, and she'd answer her cup of tepid tea, spilling it down her back. Everyone was asked to whisper in her presence, so they wouldn't wake the baby.

There was no baby.

Her mother made it through Christmas. The miracle that year, if it could be thought of as such, was that Mrs. Mun was lucid most of the morning, and she even had the strength to unwrap her gifts.

The priest came the following day. Kelly couldn't stand to watch him praying over her mother. Whether it was Kelly's own lack of interest in the church or else the nauseous reality that her mother was almost gone, she didn't stay while the priest gave her mother blessings.

She wandered into the woods on her parents' land. Old habits being what they were, Kelly brought an image of St. Jude and an image of her favorite saint from childhood, Brigid. She heard somewhere that Brigid was never even a real person; she was a Celtic goddess canonized to help convert the pagan Irish. Who knew if any of the saints were real people anyway. The church would canonize a dog in the Middle Ages and say the animal sang hymns.

Kelly knelt at the base of a juniper tree. Arranging the two little icons, she first prayed to St. Jude. Luckily, a suggested prayer was written out on the back of the card, albeit in Spanish. Kelly worked with what she had. Jude was the patron of lost hope. He probably had a soft spot in his heart for mispronounced and best-try petitions.

What you do unto the least of these, you do unto me.

Christ's words came to her unbidden, but they were the exact comfort she needed. She recalled her mother and her father reading those words to her in childhood. "The least of these."

Kelly had felt like she was less than everyone else for most of her life. "Come on, Jesus. Come on, Jude," she whispered, not knowing why she spoke so softly when she was alone in the woods. Perhaps she expected meekness to work better than boldness.

She shifted to a cross-legged position and addressed St. Brigid, trying to remember the prayer, but some soft voice in her body told her to just wing it. She reached deep into her grief and started speaking in something akin to tongues, but all the words made sense as she heard what emerged from her mouth.

"Kind and benevolent Saint Brigid, grandmother of my grandmothers, mother of the waters, queen of chalices, melter of the ice, I beseech you. By the blood of my mother, I beseech you. By the blood of my ancestors, I beseech you to heal my mother and restore her to health and sanity."

Kelly felt an overpowering compulsion to cut herself, the way she used to as a teenager, but this time she cut for a different kind of relief. She bit her thumb, but pain stopped her from breaking the skin. Kelly wondered if her emotional pain was enough to wake a goddess or if physical pain was required.

She drew out the pocketknife she always carried in those days for protection. Without hesitation, she slit the ball of her thumb and squeezed it until the red oozed and gathered enough to drip.

"By the pricking of my thumbs, something Brigid this way comes."

It was silly. Pathetic, really. But she said it anyway. It couldn't possibly make the situation worse.

She dropped a few milliliters of blood onto the ground. She felt embarrassed and ashamed, a grown woman acting like a little girl playing pretend in the woods. Being the witch instead of the princess. She wiped her thumb on the tree and sat back.

A crow cawed and clicked somewhere near her. An owl hooted.

More, came the command. It wasn't a voice as much as a sensation, the sensation of being pulled, something far more visceral than a voice in her head. *More blood.*

Kelly almost cut her wrist, knowing that a shallow slash across was not going to kill her, unlike a long trace along the veins of her forearm. She'd never gone that far.

Not like that. The other blood.

Kelly understood. She dropped the pocketknife and unbuttoned her jeans. She tried to work her freshly wounded thumb inside herself, but then she gave herself fully to the voice in her body. The menstrual blood came heavy, and she swept it up, blessing both her hands, rubbing onto the tree as much as she could.

She felt dizzy and lay down to rest a moment. When she recovered enough to sit up, she wondered why she'd done such a crazy thing. The shame hit her like her father's old belt and vanished. *Good riddance,* came her next thought. She felt guilty for thinking that about her dad, and then that guilt vanished too.

Yes. Good riddance, came that sensation-message inside her. She felt warm. She felt, for the first time in months, *good.*

Wandering back, she cleaned her hands at the spigot in the yard. The water felt freezing, but it was a mild winter so far, not truly that cold. She dried her hands on her jeans. It was then she remembered that her period wasn't due for two more weeks.

Kelly's mother lived another six months. In fact, her physical and mental recovery was deemed "miraculous" by the extended family. Even Critter came to visit—a rare thing at that time since the family had never really understood either of them, Critter or Kelly.

Kelly wrote off the change in her mother as merely the oncologist finding some different treatments that actually worked. When her mother died, it wasn't as a pitiful husk, babbling about phantom babies. It was by her own hand—

with dignity. A simple and intentional morphine overdose. Kelly believed it was intentional, even as much of a flagrant Catholic as her mother was. The alternatives were too much to think about.

With her mother resting in peace and her father dead for years, Kelly had no more reason to be a good girl and no more fucks to give. The seed of magic, dormant inside Kelly since childhood, had finally been watered. The occult fascination that her father had beaten out of her with a belt had never truly gone, just been stuffed deep where it wasn't easily noticed. Kelly fertilized that magic seed with her own blood, which was also her mother's blood—and that of ten thousand generations of mothers before them. Her menstrual cycle synched anew to the pagan stigmata that flowed out of her that day in the woods, and it came as predictably as a rent bill ever since.

Her clairolfaction returned. Kelly had forgotten that she could smell feelings and images as a child. She couldn't find much about it online or in old books, but she practiced and honed this rediscovered gift. She read everything she could on Brigid and blood magic. She sifted quickly through the popular stuff that aspiring witches explored in high school and college. There was something too treacly about those books, the same saccharine crap found in grocery store self-help paperbacks. At least Christians had a clergy to turn to for something deeper and more toothsome than that. Occultists were mostly on their own.

So she taught herself. She blew through the self-important tomes of Crowley and Grant and LaVey, the "master races" of Blavatsky and her descendants, and all the toxic positivity of the New Age, and she came back around to a mix of folk hoodoo and urban esoterica. She eventually gave up on being any kind of serious witch. She never found a demon whose ass was worth licking in return for secret knowledge. But she'd always had a knack for divination and oracle work, and the more tools she tried, the better she got.

And then, in a season when she was feeling particularly unstoppable, she met Ben.

Monday, January 6

After three days in the safe house, Kelly and Critter were starting to crack.

"I'd just as soon take my chances out there. I'd rather be eaten by spine crabs or goat spiders than just sit here reading the tarot for the thousandth time."

Kelly sat at the only table, eating her fifth bowl of cereal that day. "I'm going to relapse if I don't get out of here."

"Girl, don't even joke about that." Critter pulled a small breath from his vapor wand, clueless to the irony. "If you start fucking around with pills again, you'll probably die, and I'm not ready for you to be dead. At best, you'll be a complete cuntdragon because you're constipated again like a junkie, and I will never, ever glove up and dig you out again. That was a one-time thing. I will check you into in-patient on my own nonexistent savings before that happens."

Kelly held up her middle finger at him, but he wasn't looking. "And you'll never let me forget it. Thanks, by the way. For the millionth time. That was the greatest act of love anyone's ever shown me."

She meant it, and she hoped Critter knew she meant it. Luckily, the breakthrough that they'd been waiting for came in like a bird through window glass.

"We've got it. Finally." Detective Aweke wasn't even through the door by the end of his statement.

Kelly and Critter both perked right up. Critter dropped his wand, and Kelly pushed her bowl away. "A new body?"

"Not just a new body, though we do have one of those. We've got bardo."

Things had changed while they were cloaked and hiding out. Aweke fumed in the car about how Martinetti went over his head in the police department, arranging for the newest evidence to disappear into her own custody before the police or feds could get it. Kelly thought that whatever combination of witchcraft and political influence Sophia Martinetti wielded, they'd only seen a fragment.

"I'll be the first to admit this wasn't easy," Martinetti told them. They stood in a private laboratory and looked at the newest grotesquery that bardo had created. "It's moderately difficult to make a living person disappear in the free world. For some reason, it's far more difficult to make a dead body vanish. Didn't know until I tried."

Martinetti babbled on as usual. A bleached-blond man was with her, wearing a sterile-looking lab coat and speaking only when spoken to. Martinetti never introduced him, just directed him around.

"So is it a dryad? A treant?" Critter asked. This body was more fully transformed. It could be incidental, or it could mean that the bardo product itself was changing. The others retained their original bodies, but this one was barely human. The whole corpse was covered in tree bark, complete with lichens and moss clinging to it. What would've been the legs looked more like two tree trunks grown together. Patches of bark had sloughed off, showing the bloody human muscle underneath, like an anatomical illustration. The trunk of the body had sprouted branches, not just two "arms" but limbs upon limbs, and some of them looked more like antlers or outright bones. A single human eye, dimmed and glazed by death, lay open on one "shoulder." There was no human face but rather the suggestion of a face arranged in flowers. By the look of them, they were crocuses. Signs of spring.

As if to mock nature, the creature's penis was perfectly intact, unblemished, and very human. The whole thing was a mess. That scrambled body had fought itself, the botanical and the mammalian battling to dominate the cellular turf. That smelled like a clue. All these deaths were messy, but were they meant to be?

"Folkloric taxonomy is your specialty, Critter," Martinetti said. "When it was found, it was still moving, though immobile. It was screaming and trying to root itself in the soil. Right there in Carkeek Park. Must've scared the dogshit out of whoever saw it before we got there. Some tent people were talking about it, saying they'd seen a monster. Word travels quickly among the homeless."

Aweke jumped into the conversation, unasked. "So you sent in your goons and made it look like a police sweep. I'm not touching this at the precinct. You can clean up your own mess."

"It's already clean, Julian. Don't get cold feet now. We're finally onto something."

The tree-thing was both pitiful and frightening. The big blue eye stared, bloody sap leaking like tears. It smelled like bardo, like the *idea* of bardo that was hovering over the city, but it also smelled like sex and hope and light. For a creature that appeared to have suffered, light and hope were very odd scents to detect. The hope of the end of suffering? That didn't smell quite right.

Critter inched closer to Kelly. "Are you positive it's dead?"

Martinetti laughed so hard in the quiet room that it made Kelly jump. "Of course not! I'm not positive of anything. That's why we're all here, dumbass."

Kelly stifled a giggle. Martinetti did have a way with words.

Critter clucked his tongue against the roof of his mouth with an unnecessarily loud snap. "Voodoo spirits, Mayan goddesses, Lovecraftian entities, now. . . whatever this is. Lauma? Leshy?" Critter said.

"Are those fakelore goddesses?" Kelly asked.

Critter chewed his lower lip. "I think they're living folklore. Leshy is usually male, but Lauma is definitely female. They're both from Eastern Europe. I forget where exactly."

Something blazed in Kelly's clairolfaction. Something about Eastern Europe. The words smelled very green, like spring. "Look those up, would you? We're onto something."

Detective Aweke pulled rank. "Enough from the Wonder Twins—"

"Cousins!" they insisted in unison. Kelly took the hint and said, "But you did find bardo?"

"Yes indeed," Martinetti said. "The genuine article. That sweep of the encampment was productive, despite Detective Aweke's whining. Several of the residents are being questioned elsewhere."

Kelly grit her teeth then said, "Interrogated, you mean."

Martinetti made a *tsk*. "For god's sake, Kelly, no one's getting waterboarded. A hot meal and a fix is enough to get most of them talking. We'll even give them a shower and some new clothes."

Kelly's stomach churned. *A fix is enough.*

"In fact, most of them, I dare say, will be in better shape when they leave than when we brought them in. But yes, the bardo—"

She walked them into the next room. If Harriet's campus lab was modest by academic standards, this place used a whole other form of currency. The mix of lab equipment and computers was expected, but all the alchemical paraphernalia was not. On one table, chunky slabs of crystal sat embedded in a nest of wires. On another, samples of some kind developed under the glow of a globe that contained bioluminescent jellyfish.

The weirdest apparatus—and that was saying a lot—looked like an ornate carousel. A ring of bell jars each held a live leech in a clear liquid. In the center of the ring, floating in mid-air, was a glass Platonic prism of fitted hexagons. It reminded Kelly of a twenty-sided die. Inside, snails traveled on repeating trails of mucus, one mollusk on each of the hexagonal faces.

"Is this a real leech prognosticator?" Critter said, squatting to get a closer look.

"Get away from that," Martinetti said. "It's a combination tempest prognosticator and sympathetic compass. We're seeing if we can get the snails to mate with the leeches."

"To what end?" Kelly asked.

"To hybridize them, of course." Martinetti gave her a look as though the answer were obvious. Again with that word, *hybridize*. She'd check into any connections to the Biomes later. The whole setup looked like a child's notion of low-budget science fiction. What the hell did they do here? Throw esoteric spaghetti against a magic wall and painstakingly record the slopping noises?

"Here it is." Martinetti showed them to a table. The blank surface held a plastic sandwich bag containing a few shiny red pills and nothing else. It stuck out in a room full of esoterica.

"Have you run any tests yet?" Kelly asked.

"Only routine observation. We haven't even taken them out of the bag."

"And you're sure it's bardo?"

"A good researcher shouldn't make assumptions, but I'm certain it's bardo. The person who had it in her tent said it was called bardo, and she said her boyfriend ate it and then disappeared when he went to relieve himself in the woods. She also said her boyfriend had a tattoo of an eye on his right shoulder. Same place as the eye on that whatever-it-is strapped down in the next room."

Aweke went on. "Did the woman from the encampment say anything else about bardo? Did she take any?"

Martinetti pulled on nitrile gloves and then lifted the bag of capsules up to the light. "She said she was too afraid to take it. But she said that the man who sold it to her boyfriend was someone she'd never seen before, not a resident of the tents. She gave a description, but he could be anyone. Medium height. Dark hair. Et cetera. One curious thing she did say was that the man told her boyfriend, 'This is a dream.' That the pills were a dream."

Aweke gloved up as well and took a turn staring at them in the light. "A dream, huh? Not each one a dream, but the whole batch was a single dream?"

"If you want to be strictly literal, yes, that is what the woman said."

"I wonder if they're hallucinogenic. Or if they make you sleep. Or both. They just look like pills to me. Like liquid-gels."

"Okay, people, what do we know?" Martinetti was strangely comfortable in a laboratory. Her corporate bitch routine fell away for a few moments, and Kelly deduced that Martinetti had at one point been a laboratory researcher herself.

The anonymous assistant said, "According to Detective Mun and her sources, the bardo causes an unstable state of reality when ingested. Previously severed limbs can return and then vanish again. Wildly unpredictable physical mutations occur—but not every time. The hanged victim had no physical abnormalities. The autopsy confirmed that. The existing mutations have led, every time, to the death of the subject—except for the first girl, who came back to life."

Aweke butt in. "Who's watching her, by the way?"

"Doctor Ghavami," Martinetti answered. "With support from Goldberg and the Mesembria division."

Whatever the hell a "Mesembria division" was. Kelly added, "Her name is Tonya. You said you wouldn't hurt her."

Martinetti turned an eye to Kelly. "I believe I said we didn't *need* to hurt her." She looked back at the bag of pills as it was passed around the room for inspection. "Trust me, after the trouble we went to in apprehending a dozen tent residents on municipal property, making a young middle-class woman disappear is not currently in the plan. That could change, of course. You want to protect Tonya Williams? Keep helping me and make her redundant. Right now, it's easier to leave her be and watch her from afar. Keep it that way, Kelly."

Kelly felt a chill. Was Martinetti truly that sociopathic, that the decision to hurt someone or not would come down to nothing more than convenience versus consequence? Kelly was glad she didn't sleep with Sophia when that option was on the table.

Detective Aweke added police data. "We know that whoever is dealing this drug on the streets is targeting a disparate population: party kids, train travelers, affluent gay men, homeless campers. All groups partial to recreational drug use but with not much else in common. Crime scenes include a music venue, ticketed entry; an empty warehouse, off limits to the public; and a homosexual bathhouse, paid entry."

Critter snickered. Kelly elbowed him in the ribs. Aweke grunted and continued, "And a public park, albeit one squatted on. Race, gender, and age of overdose victims do not seem, at this time, to present a pattern. No elderly victims yet, but I'd chalk that up, again, to street drug enthusiasts. Old people do prescription drugs, not club drugs."

"Dear god, you're naive," Martinetti quipped. "And we know that part of the instability of the substance is that, at least in Miss Williams's tissue sample from the incarnated phantom limb, it tends to mimic biological cells without being actual living tissue. The ichor left behind by Mr. Gomez and the—what did you call it? Shub-Niggurath? What an unfortunate thing to name an alien goddess. The ichor that they left behind behaves the same way under the microscope. We managed to isolate one of the baby monsters and some of the egg pods, but those also collapsed into the same tar after a few hours. Can we get Harriet in here?"

"On it," the blond assistant said. He left the room.

"Anything on the hanged kid? Any similar tissue samples or residue?" Kelly gazed through the bardo pills. They looked like scarlet Nyquil caplets or LSD gels, like fresh blood in the light. They even smelled like human blood—but not exactly. The metallic tang and ancestral histories in human blood were dampened, mingled with something else difficult for Kelly to identify. Like everything else about this case, this bardo smelled like something entirely otherworldly that attempted nonetheless to appear canny.

"Nope. The kid didn't even have anything weird in his blood. The body was completely uncompromised other than that incorporeal noose. Even that part is inconsistent across the victims."

You know me.

Kelly heard the voice that came from inside her body. The one she'd heard that day in the woods as she offered her lifeblood to Brigid. Here she was.

You know me.

This spirit, so blunt yet still so vague. Kelly took a deep breath and listened to the voice.

You know. You know.

And then she did know. She knew what bardo really was, but that only made things more confusing. She kept the revelation to herself.

Harriet walked in, dressed in a lab coat and hair net. "Oh. Of course, it's you two. I wondered why there was a dead tree spirit in the other room."

Critter gave Kelly that "gritted-teeth emoji" look.

Dead trees, new flowers, Kelly thought. *The wheel of the year.* Then she asked the room, "Does anyone know of fakelore about spring? Like a fake goddess of spring?"

"Ostara! Eoster!" Critter shouted, making a few of them jump. "Easter? Goddess of Spring and Eastern Dawn?"

It smelled bang-on to Kelly. Critter launched into his infodump: "People want to reclaim the Easter holiday as pagan, but there's only like one reference to the goddess Eoster in all of the surviving texts—"

"Great," Martinetti cut him off. "So we know who this one is. Kelly, how's your nose?"

Critter took the hint and started to look things up on his phone instead of talking.

"Smells like the right lead to me. Sophia, I would like you to tell me what you find out as soon as you run your tests on the bardo samples. Meanwhile, I need some. I'm going to run it by another source. I assume Aweke and others will be keeping an eye on me as usual."

A new look came over Sophia Martinetti's face, something Kelly had never seen on the woman before. She looked afraid. Martinetti froze for a moment and then regained her cool.

"You may have *one*. Use it wisely."

"I need at least two."

"One. And then come back and we'll cross reference our findings."

With steel tweezers, Martinetti's assistant removed a single bardo pill from the bag and put it into another.

"And Kelly, don't get murdered by demons. I need you."

Kelly somehow convinced Aweke to wait in the car while she went up the wooden stairs and into the private acupuncture clinic. Aweke, ever the cop, leaned against the steering column with his arms crossed, sporting *Men in Black*-style sunglasses and staring at her. Kelly waved at him as she walked into the office of her ex-boyfriend and former oxycontin supplier, Dr. Benjamin Wei.

"Do you have an appointment?" the boy behind the counter asked.

"Nope. Walk-in."

"Okay. Dr. Wei is with patients all day, but I think I can squeeze you in if there's a cancellation."

"I'm a former patient. My name is Kelly Mun. I really, really need to see Ben today."

The receptionist looked pensive, but he handed her the intake forms on a clipboard. "If it's been more than six months since the doctor has seen you, we just need you to fill this out again. Just to keep the records up to date."

"Sure," Kelly told him and sat down in the otherwise empty lobby.

"And if it's urgent, may I let him know the reason for your visit today?"

Kelly threw out the first thought that came to mind. "Um. Menstrual cycle."

The receptionist was unfazed. "Okie dokie. Dr. Wei sees a lot of patients for that. Do you need anything for pain or mobility?" He gestured to her cottonwood cane.

"Sure, that'd be great."

"Let me see what I can do to get you on today's schedule."

For half an hour, she sat alone and made-up information for the intake forms.

Reason for visit: Menstrual cycle.

Do you have a family history of this condition: On my mother's side.

She laughed at her own joke. A patient emerged from the hallway to the treatment rooms, checked out, and left.

Everything ok? Aweke texted.

Yeah, still waiting.

"It's your lucky day. Looks like we have a no-show," the receptionist said. "Dr. Wei will be with you in a minute."

Kelly breathed with intention, steeling herself for the reunion. Ben would see her name on the forms. It wouldn't be a total shock to see her after years of mutual avoidance.

"Kelly. Come on back." He stood there in the doorway, crisp white coat over wine-red scrubs. He looked healthy. Sober. But he smelled like love and pain.

She got up and followed him. In the treatment room, they each waited for the other to speak.

"Okay, I'll start. It's good to see you, Kelly. You look well. I never expected you to come see me for anything medical, but I'd be happy to help."

He didn't look happy. She assumed that she didn't look too chipper herself.

"It's help I need, Ben. I . . . didn't want to come here. Critter encouraged me."

Ben raised his eyebrows. "Critter? How is he? Still out there chasing jiuweihu, or has he settled down?" It sounded like an insult, but it smelled like genuine curiosity.

"He's fine, Ben. I think he's dating a were-axolotl these days, but I'm sure he wouldn't turn down a gumiho. He got his degree, and now he works with me doing research. I'm a private investigator now."

Ben went stone-faced. "You're a PI with a history of addiction. Kinda cliché, isn't it?"

That was definitely a barb, and she shot back without remorse. "Like a doctor with a pill problem? Or a Chinese opiate addict?"

He smiled, and even though he looked robust, his eyes were as tired as ever. "Taiwanese. But you're not wrong. They took away my license after you left. I'm lucky to have a certificate and a private practice doing traditional Chinese medicine. I apologize for lapsing into old habits and picking a fight."

"Have you done Step Nine yet? Sounds like you have, but I don't recall you reaching out for amends."

"Nor I you. The way things ended, it seemed like contacting you to clear my conscience was just going to cause further harm. And I figured, if you stuck with recovery, maybe you felt exactly the same way about contacting me. Is that why you're here?"

"No, sorry. I think we could make amends, but . . . not right now. Not like this, and not today."

He relaxed and leaned back into his chair. "All right. So what can I do to help you today? I kind of get the impression you're not actually here about fertility or cramps, though if you are I'm . . . honored?"

"Yes and no. The occult business just gets weirder. I'm here to ask you for information. I'm on a case, and drugs are involved."

He closed his eyes and groaned. "I try so hard to stay clean and sober, Kelly. I don't even want to talk about any medicine that my zŭmŭ couldn't grow in her garden."

"That's just it, Ben. This isn't like anything I've ever seen, and I thought I'd seen everything. It's a new kind of alchemy. And it's evil. I need to talk to someone who understands more than I do about pharmaceuticals and esoteric medicine."

Ben was silent. He kept his eyes closed as Kelly waited for his response. Finally, he said, "Okay, but this is part of the amends. Amends starts here, and if you endanger my life, it ends here too. I would expect the same if our roles were reversed."

Kelly asked him if he had ever heard of bardo. He hadn't. She asked if he knew about the incidents at the Deep or at Steampipe. He had no idea.

"Okay. They look like blood, but they aren't exactly. At least, not human or animal blood. Like someone had a dream of blood, and you stole that dream and put it in a pill. And it kills people, but it kills them differently every time. It's magic in pill form."

"Kelly, I believe in a lot of esoteric stuff. Energetic medicine. I wear red for chun jié. I even believe in Chinese astrology—though not the Greek stuff. How silly is that? But I am, at heart, a doctor. And you're not even talking about superstitions that could be measured empirically. You're talking in nonsense. Poetry."

"Listen. That's just it. Poetry, dreams, things that don't make any sense. There's a lot of really opaque stuff here. It runs very deep into the occult, and there's, like, cloaks around cloaks. A lot of things masquerading as other things but not quite pulling it off. Do you know of any substance, made in a lab or wild crafted, that is anything like this?"

He did that thing that always drove her crazy where he would think way too long about something before answering her question. She thought maybe it was the narcotics that slowed him down back then. Maybe the side effect was permanent.

"I'm thinking about all the herbs and treatments I know of connected to blood, but everything's connected to blood. Blood moves the medicine around. And the things I'd prescribe specifically to help with circulation don't sound anything like what you're talking about. So at least I can confirm that just looking like blood and smelling like blood doesn't mean it's blood."

"Right. It's not real blood. It's the *idea* of blood."

"Again with the poetry. It would help if I could look at it under a microscope."

"Got one handy?"

"You know, it just so happens that I do."

It was too impractical for Ben to have a laboratory of his own. Anything he needed to test was easy to send out, and apothecary preparations were easy to ship in. Nonetheless, he had some nostalgic tools he kept in the clinic. He led Kelly back to a tiny office, just as cluttered as ever.

"Does having this stuff around make you feel like you're still a doctor?" She knew as soon as she asked that it was a shitty thing to say. "Sorry. I'm still a jerk apparently."

"I *am* still a doctor. I guess this was just the path I was destined for all along. Trust a higher power, right? Western pharmacy turned out to be a temptation I couldn't resist."

Kelly laughed. "Now who's talking in poetry? Do you think we fought so much because we're so alike?"

Ben took the plastic cover off the microscope and started fiddling with it. "I think we fought so much because we were junkies, Kelly. Oh, by the way, let me take your vitals."

Kelly recoiled as much as she could in the closet-sized office. "Ew, why?"

Ben gave her a pleading look. "You came to me, remember? Give me your wrist."

He used three fingers to check her pulse and then looked at her fingernails and her tongue. Lastly, he used the stethoscope on her heart and lungs. She let him place the cold metal against her sternum and on her back, under her shirt. Despite the hundred times he'd held her breasts and kissed her shoulders, the touch was purely clinical. Kelly wasn't sure whether that was better or worse than if he had caressed her.

"Heart sounds good. Lungs are strong but too cold."

"It's January in Seattle. I'm phlegmy."

"Your tongue has me concerned. There's too much water and wood in you, not enough metal or fire. I think your earth is fine. But your yang is really low. I want you to eat more ginger and burdock."

"Okay, that's nonsense. Next, you'll prescribe I have sex with more men on tanning beds."

"Says the woman who uses tarot to find her missing keys. You should keep your keys with your tarot cards. Now, here. I need a drop of your blood."

He opened a little sealed envelope and removed a tiny device for pricking the fingertip.

"No, I'm still needle shy. Why do you need my blood?"

"Comparison. Look, I'll do it too."

He jabbed his finger and collected the blood in a thread-thin straw, smaller than what would come in a box of ginseng ampules. He put a circular bandage on the puncture and then spread a few drops on a slide. Kelly let him swab her finger with alcohol and prick it, jumping when the little device clicked and stuck her. Ben gave her a bandage dot and prepared another slide.

"Okay, side by side. More or less. My blood, your blood, they look the same. Human blood. Although your red cell count looks slightly low. Are you eating enough?"

She blushed. "You didn't notice I've gained fifteen pounds since we broke up?"

He smiled. "Not the same question, but I'll take that as a 'yes, mostly.' And cold food in the morning or hot?"

"Whatever I want. Cold cereal. Hot coffee."

"No more cold liquids in the morning. You'll get cramps."

"You're a doctor, and you believe that?"

"Just saying. All right, now that we both know what blood is supposed to look like, let's look at one of these bardo things."

She handed him the little zip baggie, and he opened it. "Oh no, Ben, glove up. You haven't seen what that stuff does to people. I have zero idea of what it does on skin contact, but I expect it to be bad. And be frugal—it's my only sample."

He gave her that look she remembered, and then he put on his gloves and used an acupuncture needle to perforate the gel capsule. She saw the miniscule needle go in, but no liquid came out at first. Ben squeezed it very gently, and then the red contents just oozed out. It glinted in the yellowed fluorescent light from overhead.

No, it sparkled.

Kelly shut the window blinds and flipped off the light. The bardo stuff was iridescent, shimmering faintly with its own inherent light. Maybe it was vampire blood.

"Well. That's disconcerting," Ben said.

"Yeah, no shit. I am positive that this is concentrated magic. Someone has distilled it into physical stuff, and they're testing it on the streets. It's only been a few weeks, or so I've been informed by my sources. But no one I talk to knows what it is—I only just put it together myself—and absolutely no one can tell me who's making it, where, or why. I assume it's local."

Ben looked into the eyepiece of the microscope. "Huh," he grunted.

"What's 'huh'?"

"Hold on. I need a minute." He fiddled with the focus of the instrument and chewed on the whiskers just beneath his lips. Kelly always thought it was cute when he did that, but he only did it when he was worried.

"Kelly, look in here and tell me what you see."

She bent down to the eyepiece and took a second for her vision to adjust. It wasn't like the ectoplasm she'd seen in Harriet's student lab. This substance could barely be described. It was somewhat like looking at a liquid light show, the kind of colorful mineral oil displays that bands used to use in live concerts in the 60s and 70s. The globs of color seemed to move with their own will, like amoebas, yet synchronized; one unified willpower seemed to guide all the swirling color. It reminded her also of what she saw through the amber bead at Steampipe—but glittering, more of a heterogenous liquid than the vaporous energies she saw at that crime scene.

It hurt her to look at it, physically as well as emotionally. She felt something like yearning, but a specific yearning for something she would never have.

"Kelly, can you describe what you see in there?"

She tried, but everything came out in mixed metaphors.

"You can't define it, can you?" Ben asked. She shook her head and became frustrated. "I can't seem to name it either. I even find it difficult to remember what I just saw without looking again."

Cloaks around cloaks. Magic wrapped in magic. Who would sell concentrated magic to ordinary, unknowing people? Was Tonya a test subject? Why not stay cloaked and just do human testing in a private lab? There was still no pattern, no sense, no logic. Then again, magic never needed much logic. Chaos magic in particular ran on its own aethereal momentum.

"If it's magic, then we're out of our league, Kelly." Ben leaned his bony ass against the desk and rubbed his eyes.

"Everyone says that lately. I've been out of my league since I started working on this. Doesn't seem to matter. I'd probably be dead by now if I trusted pure logic rather than some higher power."

Something tugged at her when she said that. Not even her inner voice or Brigid's voice or whatever it was that told her she knew that bardo was literal magic in liquid form. It was a lurch, like a muscle spasm deep in her core. Her leg stopped tingling entirely.

"I have to go, Ben." She took the bardo slide from the microscope and sealed in in the little baggie with the perforated bardo capsule.

"Wait, what? You're just gonna leave? Did you at least get what you came to me for?"

"I-I don't know. Yes? All I know is I have to leave. Right now. I'll call you later." She hightailed it out of the little office nook, through the lobby and out the door. She could apologize later, if Ben would accept it. Right now, she felt like if she didn't leave the location immediately then she'd be in mortal danger.

Aweke was right where she left him. "Start the car," she shouted as she hugged the banister and came down the stairs. The detective did so, and Kelly got in. "Just drive. Take me somewhere safe." As they put the miles between themselves and Ben's clinic, Kelly felt the visceral pull inside her resolving. Her psychic gut intuition was becoming more acute, or the dangers were becoming more powerful.

"Wanna tell me what that was all about?" Julian said after a while.

"I don't know. I don't know. I just had to . . . get away." The car paused at a red light on 36th and Phinney. She gazed out the window at crows fighting over a dead squirrel. More joined them, and as Kelly watched the tussle, the crows became violent. They pecked at each other's eyes and slashed with their claws. The birds became a small cloud of black feathers and blood, an explosion of rage and hatred the likes of which she had never seen, even among humans. She could smell their blood even with the car windows up.

Things were *off*. The portents were too garish to ignore.

The light turned green. Kelly watched the overcast sky through her passenger window. Something was wrong with the clouds. They behaved like the bardo under the microscope, indefinable and terrifying and miraculous all at once.

It began to rain blood. The fine red mist glistened on the windshield and then became a full downpour. People on the sidewalks panicked and screamed.

"Now you going to tell me what the hell is going on?"

"Keep driving. Carefully. Seattleites can't even drive in regular rain. Just get us back to Martinetti's lab. I think we must be extremely close to finding out where bardo is made and who's making it. The signs are all here that we've pierced their cloaking spells. The birds going crazy. The red rain. Some heavy magic is waking up."

She got an email on her phone: *You okay Kelly?*

Ben was worried about her. He sent her his contact info. She called him as Aweke wove through the other drivers who lost their collective shit in the scarlet rain.

"Hey, Ben. Thank you, I'm fine. Um, is it raining where you are?"

"Not right now. Oh, yeah, it's starting. Holy mother of Christ—"

"Yeaaah," Kelly sighed. "There's some really heavy energies moving through the city."

"No shit, Kel. Is this why you rushed out?"

She looked at Aweke, but he was entirely focused on predicting and evading other drivers' bad decisions.

"Yes and no. Look, Ben, please be very careful for the next few days. Use all your protective charms. Herbs, feng shui, saints, ancestors, gods, all of it. Hell's breaking loose, and I have no idea which hell it is."

"Listen, I was going to mention while you were here. Um. I'm sober right now, but I had a short relapse last year. I got mixed up with some weird shit."

Kelly's nostrils flared. She now smelled the horrible vomit stench of the spine crabs—not bardo, not the indefinable scent resting over Seattle like a fog, but the hot, electric, demonic odor of pure evil. It seemed to come through the phone.

"Ben, what are you telling me? This is very important. Are you in danger? Am I?"

"I don't think so, Kel. But I don't know. There's a guy somewhere in Seattle called Dr. Leng. No idea if that's his real name. I never met him, but something about this bardo situation makes me think he could be involved. He's some kind of local kingpin, imports a lot of the fentanyl. Or he did recently. My dealer wanted to introduce me, said Leng was interested in fusing w⊠xing and alchemy with the newer designer drugs. I was screwed up enough to actually consider it. But the next time I met my dealer, she said I should forget about him. Don't even talk about him. Then she died of a fentanyl overdose. I think Leng had her killed. And bardo sounds a lot like what he was working on."

Kelly wrapped up the conversation as Detective Aweke pulled the car into an underground garage. "Stay safe. I . . . Ben, I . . ."

"You love me? I love you too, Kelly. Protect yourself."

Ben ended the call. She did love him, after everything. She loved him like she loved Critter, and that was perfect.

"So," Aweke said as they got out of the car. "What was that all about?"

"New lead. Have you ever heard of a Dr. Leng?"

Aweke went quiet for a long moment and then said, "Leng? *L-e-n-g*?"

"I think that's the name. Could doublecheck."

"Leng's a nasty hyena of a man. I think Martinetti worked with him years ago. What about him?"

"My contact said he thinks Leng may be involved. Is he still in Seattle?"

Aweke laughed but not with mirth. "Dr. Leng has been dead for nearly a year. Shot in a police raid."

Something smelled off. Not like a lie but like another cloak.

"Are you absolutely sure he's dead?"

Aweke laughed again. "I'm sure. I put the bullet through his head myself."

A chill passed through Kelly. "Let's get upstairs and debrief with Sophia."

THE ABOMINABLE DR. LENG

KELLY, CRITTER, AWEKE, AND SOPHIA CROWDED AROUND THE VIDEO screen in her office. The feed showed a first-person view entering a mausoleum. Some of Sophia's occult science goons streamed the exhumation in progress.

After the raid, Leng's body was identified by a woman claiming to be his sister. God only knew who she actually was. The casket was transferred to Los Angeles for burial but "lost" along the way. So was the sister.

That was the official story. According to Julian, the paper trail was tweaked to look like the woman requested full privacy to bury her brother and then disappeared into her private life. Although the trail was cold, it was no difficulty for Sophia's people to find the tomb where Abraham Leng's final resting place had been registered. Turned out it really was in LA.

Kelly knew what Martinetti's people would find inside the casket, and she also knew to keep her commentary to herself right about now.

Sophia stared at the screen with rage in her eyes. Her employees, or whatever they were, cracked through the public-facing marble wall of the niche, revealing the casket inside. So far nothing unusual. The small team hefted the casket out and onto the floor. They had to work hard and fast to get it open; a binding spell made some of their tools break before they penetrated the field.

The team was not informed of why they had this assignment, just to do the task and report and record everything. Where they expected to find either a dead body or an empty crypt, instead they found more black goo. Sophia said, "Put it back in the wall and make it all go away." She raised the little white remote to end the call, paused, and said, "And I want each of you to piss in it before you close it up." She shut off the feed.

"Was it really necessary," Aweke asked, "to embarrass your team like that?"

"We need to break down his power. It's necessary if I say it's necessary. Like I told you it was necessary to kill Leng."

"He was *dead*. Three shots to the chest and one to the forehead," Detective Aweke reassured Sophia. "No way someone could have saved him. Even with magic."

"Obviously, the man you thought you killed was never really alive." Martinetti spun a huge, pointed chunk of amethyst on her desk. It balanced like a blade.

"I killed Dr. Abraham Leng," Detective Aweke insisted. "I killed a flesh-and-blood man."

"No, Julian, you 'killed' a golem of Dr. Leng. Did you talk to him? Interact? Or did you just kick in the door, guns blazing?"

Kelly and Critter looked sidelong at one another.

"He reached for a gun, Sophia. I did my job." Aweke started going through his pockets for something, not finding it.

"Oh, like hell you did. You saw your opportunity and you capped him." Martinetti lit another cigarette. A More brand 120 this time by the look of it. "I'm not saying you did the wrong thing. I wanted you to kill him. But you killed the *wrong* him." She blew smoke out of her nostrils. "Jesus tapdancing Christ, why can't things just be easy sometimes?"

Critter smacked his lips and said, "May I speak?"

"No," Martinetti and Aweke said in unison. Critter turned his nose up and started playing with his phone.

Martinetti nursed her 120, cupping her elbow in her free hand, and continued. "No, no, this is my fault. We should've double and triple checked that he was dead. Should've had you behead him and cut out his heart like the vampire he is and then burn it all and piss in the ashes. Leng is one of the most brutal criminal alchemists on the West Coast. Big money and bigger magic. You didn't even take his vitals after you shot him in that raid."

Aweke ran a hand over his face. "I did my job. It's someone else's job to take vitals and do postmortem. Mine is to kick in doors and shoot gangsters, apparently."

Martinetti bit through the filter of her slender cigarette, and the rest of it fell to her desk. Aweke's eyes bulged. No one said a word until Martinetti stamped out her 120 and spoke.

"Julian. I am very upset that you're making me say this in front of the help—"

Critter and Kelly looked at each other again, but Kelly shook her head and brought a finger to her lips.

"—so I'll only say this once. Stay in your lane. Do what you're paid to do. If the mood strikes, fuck me now and then. You're a good lover and a great employee, but you are not my *partner*. Is that crystal clear?"

If Aweke's skin weren't so dark, Kelly was sure she would see him turn fuchsia. That's why he smelled like sex the first time she met him. He was shtupping the boss.

That escalated quickly, Kelly thought.

Critter just pursed his lips without looking up and typed—*Girl whut?*—turning his screen at a stealthy angle so Kelly could see. Sophia put her hand on Julian's. Despite his silence, she said, "I care about you too. I don't want anything to happen to you." She stood.

"And with that awkwardness over with, let's figure out where the real Dr. Leng is. He's certainly not rotting in that mausoleum. I cannot believe we fell for an ectoplasm golem. How utterly tacky." She looked out the blood-streaked window at the red Seattle cityscape. The blood rain had finally stopped. Sophia became meek. "I fell right into his ruse."

This was the first time Martinetti had shown vulnerability. She was not a woman who admitted her mistakes freely.

"Sophia, I think we know everything we need now to zero in on him." Kelly pulled out her tablet and started to free associate.

Leng. Ben. Blood rain. Sparkle.
Golem. Ectoplasm. Ichor. Shub-Niggurath.
Garuda. Bahama. Come on pretty mama.
Dead of wet winter. Steam. Pipes. Rain.
Silver Ash Cure. Maggot. Steam. Blood.
Spine crabs. Hanged Man. Gallows. Intact.
Easter. Wheel of the Year. Park sweep. Killer pill.
Tania. Arms. In the arms of the Bardo.
The arms of my mother. The arms of Brigid.

She ran the cut-up generator with a factor of three. The program spat out:

Pill. Tania. Arms. Pill. Tania. Arms. Rain. Sparkle. Golem. Rain. Sparkle. Golem. Of the Bardo. Of the Bardo. The arms of my mother. Of my mother. The Come on pretty Leng. On pretty Leng. Ben. Blood wet winter. Blood wet winter. Steam. Niggurath. Garuda. Steam. Niggurath. Garuda. Bahama. Easter. Park sweep. Bahama. Golem wheel. Park sweep. Killer Cure. Maggot. Killer Cure. Maggot. Steam. Pipes. Silver Ash Ectoplasm. Silver Ash Ectoplasm. Ichor. Shub Spine crabs. Shub Spine crabs. Hanged mama. Dead of In the arms Man. The arms Man. Gallows. Intact.

She highlighted the phrases that stuck out to her and copied them down to another field:

Rain sparkle golem of the bardo.
Come on pretty Leng.
Blood wet winter.
Hanged mama.
Killer cure.
The arms man. Gallows intact.

"Anything?" Critter asked.

"Shhh, working." The tablet blinked out and bricked. "Dammit!" Kelly said, shaking it like an etch-a-sketch and then digging in her bag for a charger cord.

Martinetti inhaled loudly and said, "Don't bother. It's probably part of his cloaking spell. Tech isn't going to do much to assist us. Not with blood raining from the sky."

Cloaking, Kelly thought. *How do I pierce the cloak?*

"We need to find the epicenter," Kelly told them. "I think he's getting his raw magical material from the other side of the veil and then turning it into bardo. He's going to be in a place where the walls between worlds are thin or nonexistent. Where are the closest soft places?"

"In Seattle?" Martinetti lit another fancy cig. "That could be anywhere."

"I'm serious, Sophia. We're chin-deep in shit. You're way too smart to be this glib right now."

Martinetti looked furious for less than a second and said, "You're right. I'm . . . afraid. Afraid that I'm out of my league here."

For a moment, Kelly felt sorry for her.

Sophia Martinetti continued. "I need everyone's help to close this little account. I thought Leng was just a drug lord, but then he started becoming a threat to the occult market. I respected the man as a shrewd rival. Sure, I tried to have him murdered, but that's practically a compliment coming from me. He ran a pretty clean racket in the drug trade—until he didn't. He started getting into human trafficking and then occult weapons. Went a bit crazy, started screwing up the whole delicate ecosystem of the occult trade. Got messy, killed some of my people. So yeah. I arranged for Julian to kill him in a raid."

She put her hand on Detective Aweke's shoulder. He didn't flinch. "I'm sorry. This is my fault, not yours. For all your peccadilloes, you're a good cop, and you're mixed up with a bad woman like me."

The two of them were living in their own private noir movie. Aweke kissed her hand. Critter looked touched. Men fell for anything.

Kelly was not as moved. "'Sorry' isn't going to cut it, I'm afraid. We need to act right now."

Martinetti frowned. "Just clearing the pipes, dear."

Pipes, Kelly thought. She smelled rust and steam and bardo.

"Leng's as afraid of us as we are of him." Critter unwrapped a green jolly rancher and popped it in his mouth. Everyone looked at him. "God knows what he's doing with bardo, but he sent a demon to protect *it* from *us*. He's on the defensive, and we know he's cornered and dangerous, but he'll also be getting desperate. You said he was getting messy. Sounds like too much ambition and too much arrogance. Crazy or not, he's as out of his depth as we are. We can use this to our advantage."

Aweke said, "You know, you're a shrill little mosquito, but I'm starting to like you too."

"I'll alert the media," Critter said and cracked the candy between his back teeth.

"Critter's right," Kelly said. "We've got Leng spooked now. His magical alarms are going off. The red rain is a warning—not for us but for him. Intruder alert."

Martinetti narrowed her eyes and frowned. "So we *did* pierce the cloaking spell?"

"One of them. Several, probably. We got through the *what* and the *who*, and now all that's really cloaked is the *where*. I couldn't care less about the *why*. Maybe his mommy didn't love him enough or some misogynist bullshit like that. Let's just find his lab and . . ."

Kelly let out a huff of breath. "And . . ." She was at a loss. The other three spoke over one another:

"And we wreck it!" Critter said.

"We find out exactly how he makes bardo," Martinetti said.

"And we kill him!" Detective Aweke said.

Kelly blinked. "Wow. So . . . yeah. Let's start by figuring out the main goal. Critter and I were hired to gather information. We did the job, but now we're in the crosshairs of a maniac sorcerer. So as much as it pains me to say it, I guess I'm in this to the end. What's next, Sophia?"

Martinetti paced the room again, gesturing with an unlit cigarette. "Leng's playing with Promethean fire. Golems, demons, magic drugs . . ."

Kelly smelled something in her statement: a mix of rightness and wrongness, accuracy and inaccuracy, a scent like wood smoke and rain mingled. She closed her eyes to concentrate on her clairolfaction.

Martinetti went to a shelf and retrieved an old-fashioned cigarette lighter, the heavy bronze kind. She clicked it a couple of times until the flame rose, but then she put it down without lighting the 120.

"Let's get back to basics. A scientist, a cop, a PI, and a librarian walk into a crime scene . . ."

So she was a scientist after all. That smelled entirely accurate. She hadn't described herself just now as a businesswoman or even as the femme fatale she incessantly projected. Martinetti thought of herself as a scientist first and foremost.

Aweke spoke up. "We need to find someone who's taken bardo and lived. We're only looking at casualties—maybe overdoses—so far. Tonya seemed like a perfect lead, but she has nothing. We even sent psychics to read her. Nothing. Her story hasn't changed."

Martinetti picked up a different lighter, this one a cheap-plastic pocket kind. "Tonya's description of the man who sold her bardo matches the description of the guy who sold it to the tree-thing, at least what his girlfriend said. But that could be any goddamn guy in Seattle. Medium height, short brown hair, wearing a dark blue hoodie. There is literally nothing individual there. Could even be two different men who sold to Tonya and the tree-man."

She put her unlit cigarette to her lips and flicked the flame on the lighter. Then she grumbled and once again put down the Bic without lighting the tobacco. "Ugh. So frustrating. I guaran-damn-tee you that whoever is pushing bardo at street level is someone high-ranking in Leng's project. This isn't something you entrust to some frat boy loser at the bottom of the pyramid."

Kelly caught a whiff of sandalwood incense at the word "pyramid." Another smokey smell, but that could just be some casual synesthesia. What else would pyramids smell like? Sand?

No, beneath the brief top note of dry sandalwood was something different. A green, lush smell, like wet jungle and rich dirt. More contradictions. That had to be Ixtab: pyramids in the jungle, incense and loam. That connected back to the hanged kid, the one they never identified.

Why couldn't this just be another routine case of infidelity or insurance fraud? Those always smelled so blatantly obvious.

Martinetti was now pacing and flicking her lighter on and off.

"Would you just light that cigarette already?" Critter blurted out. "Jesus. It's like waiting for cum to dry."

Sophia laughed. "And here I thought librarians were supposed to be patient." She finally lit the cig and drew a big lungful. Critter pulled out his vapor wand and sucked it.

"I didn't say you could vape in my office."

Critter's face turned pink. "Oh. Sorry? I just figured . . ."

Kelly's concentration was thoroughly broken, so she rejoined the chatter. "Okay, so the street dealers are a dead end. We've never found anyone who took bardo and lived, besides Tonya Williams, and she's given us all the info she can. We're still behind here. Who knows how many people can take bardo and live? We don't even know what its intended effects would be. Let's look again at what we *don't* have—for one, we don't know where Leng is, but we're getting close. We still don't have an ID on the drifter kid. We know that bardo is concentrated magic, but we still don't know what processes Leng uses to either harvest or distill it."

Julian leaned forward and put his elbows on his knees and his chin in his hands. "We're also missing a motive. Drugs are always about money, but I doubt the tree guy or the hanged kid had much to spend. The drug is still in its testing stage, or else we'd be seeing more casualties with a longer lead time. And why make a drug out of pure magic? To give people . . . what? The power to cast spells? Doesn't seem like something that a megalomaniac would want to share with the world."

Then it hit Kelly like pure opium.

"Leng isn't testing the drug so he can sell it. He's testing it so he can *take it*. So he knows how to survive the experience. He has no intention to sell it on the street. He's making a magic drug just for himself."

She smelled so many things then, confirming her words. She smelled blood and fire, birth and death, pregnancy and violence, rich earth and ancient graves.

"And I think he's the one pedaling it too. From what you've told me, he's too paranoid to let someone else do it. That's why no one can remember anything significant. He's got a glamour wrapped around a cloak. He looks like everyone."

She also smelled Brigid—a scent of melting ice, misty forests, and mother's milk. She smelled Brigid, and the goddess was weak and in pain. The others' voices faded out around her. She heard the goddess's voice deep inside her womb, and the goddess said, *Help me.*

Where are you? How do I help you? Kelly asked the questions silently but with her full soul.

The broken place. With the warlock. Help me. Use the drug to find me. Then the contact faded, and Brigid was gone.

The "warlock" had to be Leng. The broken place was the epicenter they were looking for, but where the hell was it? Her growing anxiety now erupted into rage, and she blurted out, "Leng kidnapped my goddess."

The others stopped their chatter and stared at her. Critter said, "Is that another cut-up? Like, 'french toast wanders the abyss?'"

"No, I mean exactly what I said. Leng is a warlock, and he's got the goddess Brigid bound somewhere, and she said she's in the broken place."

"Another goddess," Critter bit his lower lip. "A Celtic one, appropriated as a Catholic saint. Does that count as fakelore?"

"Doesn't matter," Aweke said. "It's a lead."

Martinetti put her hand on Kelly's shoulder, an unusually gentle gesture from the queen bee. "What exactly did you figure out?"

Kelly repeated the goddess's words.

Sophia bared her teeth between her perfectly painted lips. "A soft place. A broken place . . ."

"That makes sense," Critter began. "Epicenters are soft places because the wall between realities is so thin you can slip through it. In this case, it sounds like that wall isn't just thin, it's cracked open."

Martinetti narrowed her eyes and frowned. "Yes, Critter, I'm aware of that."

"Oh," he said, straightening his posture. "Sorry for mansplaining."

"What makes a soft place 'soft'?" Julian was still hunched forward in his deductions. "What broke the wall down?"

"Trauma," Kelly said. "Pure human suffering. The psychic screams of hundreds, maybe thousands of people. It's enough unalloyed power to weaken the barrier between worlds."

"That could be anywhere," Detective Aweke said. "Tulsa, Auschwitz, Hiroshima . . ."

"But it's not just anywhere. It's here." Martinetti finally sat down behind her desk. "This whole city is a soft place, Julian. Natives pushed off their land without treaty, fires that destroyed whole neighborhoods, the heroin epidemic. Not to mention rampant homelessness, violence against immigrants . . ."

Julian grumbled. "As I said, that could be anywhere. So why here?"

"Let's backtrack," Kelly said. "How did you find Leng the first time? Where was his seat of power?"

"'Power' is exactly it," Julian said. "He was holed up in the old Georgetown steam plant. Right there in a historic building, right under our noses."

"Julian found him through good old fashioned detective work. He tailed some of Leng's thugs and found that they kept coming and going from the steam plant, though usually underground."

Something smelled off. Kelly asked, "You sure you didn't use any esoteric means to find him?"

Detective Aweke looked at Sophia. She rolled her eyes and said, "Well. He doesn't believe in it, but I also dowsed for it just to confirm. And the dowsing crystal said he was right."

"I thought dowsing was debunked after World War II," Critter said.

"Not for the British, it wasn't. The Nazis were too distracted with their World Ice theories and their Ariosophy to use dowsing to much effect. They found Mussolini and sprung him from jail, but they couldn't do jack shit when it came to dowsing over the ocean. 'Blood and soil' don't hold much power on the seas, and Germany is landlocked. The Brits, on the other hand, as an island nation, were very good at dowsing the ocean. They say Alan Turing could find a single pearl in the middle of the Pacific once he combined divination with decryption."

"More alchemy," Julian mumbled.

"And don't even get me started on Grace Hopper. Brilliant alchemist—"

Kelly let the rest of the group talk it out while she went inward. She didn't need a computer to make cut-ups. She didn't even need scissors and paper.

She concentrated on the smell of steam and let her mind go wherever it would. *Fire and water. Union of opposites. Solve et coagula. Macrocosm to microcosm. As above, so below. Alchemy. The Baphomet. The Art of Temperance. The Androgyne, the Judge, and the Hanged One.*

The images of tarot cards shuffled through her mind, like hyperphantasia in its detail.

Steampipe. Bath house. Dowse steam. Sex and water. Spider goat. Death and sex. Glory hole. Easter resurrection. Death and steam.

As she relaxed her body and her mind, the ideas and images began to blend.

Fire water unite Baphomet. Gender water. Androgyne anodyne.

So below. Below the base of the pyramid. The iceberg. The alchemy below. Brigid below.

"We need to dowse again, but this time track the steam pipes." The others stopped talking and listened to Kelly. "The pipes are the ley lines. The old steam plant was the epicenter, but it's corrupted now. If he can't use an actual steam plant, he's going to use a nexus of steam pipes."

"And that's where we'll find the soft place?" Aweke asked. "The soft place opened up at a nexus of the steam lines?"

"The steam lines will converge where soft places have opened," Critter said. "It's magic. Don't overthink it."

Kelly continued. "We're going to have to go underground. Everything is leading me to something literally underground. Or maybe underwater? No, underground for sure. I think Leng needs to be close to water to do his work, and the fire-water alchemy of the steam makes things even more powerful. That's one reason why he used to occupy the old steam plant."

"And the other reasons?" Detective Aweke asked.

Kelly closed her eyes and opened her clairsentience. It usually didn't work, but her gut told her it was the right "*clair-*" for this.

"The plant is another soft place, but it wasn't nearly as powerful as the one he's using right now. The plant was good enough to collect ectoplasm and make a golem—but not bardo. The new place is powerful enough to . . ."

She lost it for a few seconds.

"To what?" Aweke was getting salty again.

"I don't know. It's like the whole thing should be obvious. But I can't see it, only the edges of it. The cloaking spells are still holding up."

Critter said, "Well. Let's bust out a map of the steam pipes and dowse it."

The tarot imagery went through Kelly's mind again: alchemical androgynes, sacred intersex bodies. Two-spirit shamans. The unified energies of transcendent alchemy.

"Critter needs to hold the pendulum," she said.

Martinetti argued, "No, I'm the best dowser I've ever met. Critter might be fantastic, I don't know, but this is something we can't risk on a hobbyist."

"Hobbyist?! I have a master's degree in occult research!" Even incensed, he was adorable.

"No. It has to be Critter," Kelly said. "To find an epicenter, we need an *epicene*. Critter's the most genderfluid person I've ever known." She took his hand. "You bring together the opposites. Because to you, they aren't opposites. And you're the only trans person in the room. We need that energy."

"Huh," Critter said. "I'm not sure whether to be offended or flattered."

"Be both. That's what we need right now. A union of disparate energies."

Detective Aweke's phone rang. "Hello," he said with exhaustion in his voice. "What? How could you let that happen?"

Before the rest could react, Critter's phone vibrated. He looked at it and said, "It's Harriet. That's weird. She hates calling. She only texts." He put the phone to his ear and answered.

The two conversations vied for Kelly's attention. Aweke stood up and walked out of the office.

"Hey, don't yell at me, man," Critter was saying. His face didn't look angry but perplexed and fearful.

Kelly felt her phone buzz with a text in her pocket, but she ignored it. Julian came back in.

"Tonya Williams is gone. Our people had her house under surveillance around the clock, and she just disappeared. She went into her home and never came back out. No trace. No sign of struggle. Her grandmother saw nothing, and she was home the entire time."

Critter ended his call. "You guys. That was Harriet's brother. He said she vanished in a backyard swimming pool."

Martinetti raged. "Harriet? My Harriet? Oh, hell no."

Critter continued, "She dove in and never surfaced. She's just gone, and her family blames me and Kelly for getting her involved in all of this."

Martinetti went stone-faced. "More wet magic. Every time we learn something, Leng is a step ahead of us, raising the stakes."

Critter injected his typical optimism. "But every time we learn something, it breaks a cloaking spell. He's raising the stakes because we're so close. Let's get the dowsing pendulum and the maps and see if we can find him."

Kelly's phone buzzed again in her pocket. She pulled it out to find two texts from Ben: the first said only, *Help,* and the second, *INS.*

"They've got Dr. Wei," she said. She showed the messages to Aweke.

"Christ. Wei too? They're making the witnesses disappear. Tidying up the current mess. Why send INS though? Was Wei undocumented?"

"His parents immigrated, but he was born in Seattle. Now his folks are naturalized. Unless Leng messed with Ben's records."

"I wouldn't put it past him," Aweke said.

She called his office. The receptionist picked up after two rings. He told Kelly that after the blood rain let up, Ben went outside to collect samples of it and never came back. His car was still at the office, but he too had vanished.

She ended the call. "Goddammit. I guess we're gonna have to save Ben too."

Critter said, "Well he's a human being, just like Harriet and Tonya, and we have to help. Just don't get back together with him, okay?"

"Oh my god, never!" she protested.

Critter just gave her his "Bitch, please!" look.

As the others gathered the dowsing tools and argued, Kelly meditated on the images now flying around in her head. Water and rain. Blood and thuja branches. Steam. Immigrants, mostly Chinese and Japanese, standing in lines in an old jail. But there were works of art everywhere in the prison. In the stairways, painted onto windows, mosaics embedded in the floors. She saw artwork, bright and hopeful, amongst the miserable faces of incarcerated people.

She was almost there. Kelly's mind reached into the images for an epiphany. She saw the place where Ben was held along with Tonya and Harriet. It was like a museum and a prison at the same time, and that didn't even smell like a metaphor. She was seeing one location across time, but the space was fixed.

The cloaking spell was too strong. She could see the room with the hostages but not the bigger picture. She struggled to detect anything that could give away the physical location—unless the location wasn't physical.

Use the drug to find me, Brigid had said. She couldn't mean for Kelly to swallow bardo. Could she?

The others continued to distract themselves and each other from their goal. Lives were at stake, and these weren't strangers dead in a hot tub or a public park. These were people she knew. How long until Leng grabbed Rattlesnake, or even Critter?

Kelly thought about what her life really meant. *Nothing and everything,* Ji Jang or Brigid would've said. Every life precious. Every life meaningless. The beautiful, empty, terrifying freedom of life.

So she did it. Before the others could realize what she was doing and stop her, she pulled the bardo capsule out of her pocket, out of its plastic baggy, and she licked it at the little shimmery spot where Ben had pricked it with the needle.

The hit knocked her off her chair. She saw every color, felt every emotion. She thought she must be dying.

When the initial blast subsided, she had a vision. Like a cartoon that follows a drainage pipe down into the ground, past ant colonies and buried treasure chests and dead dinosaurs, she tracked a metal pipe moving down into the earth, down and down, until it reached hell. Which was unbearable.

It was pure chaos and suffering, an intersection of Dante's *Inferno* with all the Buddhist Narakas and even *Hellraiser.* Kelly felt immediately horrified, nauseated, and terrified. Her ego mind struggled to look away, but her spirit stared at the scenes with infinite compassion and courage.

Amidst the cacophony of spirits, she saw some familiar ones. Not her human allies, as she'd fearfully expected, but the goddesses and the monsters. Indigenous Ixtab, tangled in a web. Dark and beautiful Ti Kitha Demembre, the parts of her body separated into individual cages and struggling to reconnect. There was a flower-headed Eoster, and there was something atrocious that could only be Shub-Niggurath. Brigid wept in chains.

From each of these captive spirits, a nightmare of alchemical technology collected their blood. Some spirits' blood dripped from self-inflicted wounds into pans below. Others had brass and rubber tubes stitching in and out of their skin, pumping their blood like milk into canisters.

Kelly snapped out of the vision and puked onto the office floor. Martinetti recoiled, but Critter came over and held her.

Aweke just sighed. "Okay, I guess *I'll* clean that up."

Kelly spit a couple of times onto the floor and then caught her breath. "Oh god, I saw hell. They're in a hell realm—at least the goddesses are. Ti Kitha, Ixtab, all the ones we've been talking about, and others. Tonya and Harriet and Ben are somewhere else, but I think it's right on top. Somewhere that's like an art museum and a prison for immigrants at the same time. It's the soft place where the hell realm and our world touch."

Martinetti brought Kelly a glass of water. Aweke brought towels from the executive bathroom and mopped up the vomit. Mercifully, Kelly hadn't had much to eat that day, and the smell was tolerable. She thought of Ji Jang's closing advice from her vision: *That cup is dust. Only the water remains.*

"I know what bardo is now," she said.

Martinetti held the water glass for her while she recovered. "I thought you said bardo is distilled liquid magic. In gel caps."

"It is. It is. But it's a lot more than that. It's not just some abstract energy that he coagulates. It's blood. It's the blood of spirits and goddesses. *He's bleeding goddesses and selling their blood.*"

"I told you that he's a monster," Martinetti said, sitting beside Kelly and taking her hand. The gesture was kind, almost maternal, but Sophia's mouth made sure she didn't come across as too sweet.

Once the floor was clean and Kelly felt stable, they brought out the dowsing map. Critter held the gold chain of the pendulum, suspending a small shard of quartz over the tangled cartography of streets and sewers and steam lines. He started at the Georgetown Steam Plant, the previous lair where the golem was shot.

The crystal twisted like a knob at the end of the pendulum, almost playfully. "It likes you," Martinetti told Critter.

They looked for museums nearby. The pendulum didn't respond to the Museum of Flight. The Nordic Museum was also a no-go and so was the Living Computers Museum.

"This is stupid," Julian said. "What, are we going to test every museum and prison in town? How do we even know it's in Seattle?"

"Try the ICE prison down in Tacoma," Kelly said.

Martinetti bristled. "Privatized deportation. Despicable. Leng would be involved in that."

Critter looked up. "I didn't think you'd care about those things."

"I care about a lot of things. I just care about myself the most."

"Touché," Critter said and went back to the map. When the crystal hovered over the immigration detention center down south, it went taught at the end of the chain, but it swayed left and right as if to say, "No, uh-uh."

"It's not there, but we're on the right track," Martinetti told them. "Try the Wing Luke."

Critter slowly traced northward to the Chinatown International District, aiming for the Wing Luke Museum of the Asian Pacific American Experience. It was a long and specific title, and everyone in Seattle just called it the Wing Luke or the Wing.

As the crystal got close to its mark, it suddenly tugged on the chain so hard that it moved Critter's hand. The crystal pinpointed a building two blocks south of the Uwajimaya market.

"Where is that?" he asked.

Kelly and Sophia were stumped. "I have no idea," Martinetti said. "Probably an abandoned building. But that's where Leng is doing his dirtiest work."

The crystal bounced on the end of the pendulum like a child on a hotel bed.

"I know exactly where that is," Detective Aweke said. "It's the Inscape Arts Center. Bunch of offices and studio spaces for artists. But before they gutted it and turned it over to the hipsters—"

"It was the INS building," Critter said, "with its very own detention and processing center."

The crystal plunged downward and shattered against the map and the table beneath it. Everyone jumped back, but no one caught any shards. The pendulum chain was suddenly so hot in Critter's fingers that it burned him, and he dunked his fingers in Kelly's water glass.

They all just looked at one another, waiting for someone to speak.

"Alright people," Martinetti broke the silence. "We found the warlock and his secret lair. Now we need some very big juju and a tight plan."

TO BLEED A GODDESS

THE CAT HAD BEEN THE BLOW THAT CRIPPLED HER, EMOTIONALLY. KELLY and Ben had fought most venomously over the cat: who allowed helpless little Boogers to starve, whose responsibility it was to take care of her . . .

Kelly loved that damn cat more than she loved Ben. And certainly more than she loved herself. She'd grabbed all her shit—and some of Ben's—and bailed. Let him figure out the rent alone. She knew on some level that she was doing them both a favor, but in the throes of addiction, she also had the satisfaction of knowing she was shattering Ben's world.

Or maybe it was the other way around, or both. Schrödinger's Fuck-Up. Either way, the cat was still dead. Poor little Boogers.

The first time Kelly slammed morphine, she knew she was as good as dead too. *As long as I'm not injecting it, I can still stop.* Well, that warning sign had just hit her in the face and taken her head off. The tighter controls on prescription meds made it more difficult for Ben to get oxycontin and other pills, but liquid morphine was easy to make disappear. It wasn't her method of choice, but it scratched the itch under her skin. She knew the next low would be slamming street heroin and then probably dying on fentanyl. With her last scrap of self-preservation, she fled.

She stayed with Critter for a week before he kicked her out. She screamed and cried and called him horrible things she couldn't ever take back, but he was right. She was just stalling at his place and taking advantage of him. Kelly told her cousin she was stepping her dosage down and weaning herself off, but that was a lie. Was it still a lie if she was only lying to herself? That didn't matter. She broke a dozen promises in a week, and Critter wouldn't allow it to go on any longer.

Kelly bought a one-way ticket to Sedona. She had a friend there, a fling who'd passed through town right before she met Ben. Her friend told her she always had a place to stay if she cared to visit.

Compared to soggy Seattle, Arizona was like Mars. Kelly heard it was a lot easier to get sober in a new environment, far from what other addicts called the "scene of the crime." She had enough presence of mind to erase and block everyone in her phone who was part of the problem. Something nagged at her still, some unfinished business, conspicuous by its absence. She didn't figure it out until she landed in Sedona, and then she cried: she hadn't had a single clairolfactive experience in months. Zero extrasensory perception, and she hadn't even noticed. She could not remember the last time Brigid had spoken to her either. She tried to tune in, but she couldn't concentrate.

Her last stash of pills was nearly gone. She'd stolen enough cash from Ben to get a cab to Rattlesnake's house. In the cab, she texted: *Hey. It's Kelly. I'm in Sedona unexpectedly. Can I stay with you for a few days?*

Rattlesnake didn't text back until Kelly was a block away. *The door's open. Come in and clean up.*

"So you lost your magic, and now you want some of mine." Rattlesnake brewed tea for them, a blend of greenthread, nettle, and oat straw. It was good, earthy, and slightly metallic or stony, something to help dry up all of that sludge inside of her.

Kelly folded into herself, knees under her chin, while Rattlesnake whittled a stick of cottonwood.

Rattle continued. "I'm not angry. I'm just stating the reality. First, we clear the space by naming the truth. Then, we fill that space with a new medicine."

Rattlesnake always reminded Kelly of an inverted Medusa. Their thick black and silver dreadlocks ended in beads and real snakes' rattles instead of the serpent heads. Sometimes they added a few tiny bells. You could always hear Rattle coming, and that was by design. They wanted people to be ready for them.

Their gaze could freeze anyone in place. People regularly stopped talking when they walked past, hypnotized by this genderless witch with the rattling dreads. Kelly didn't know what to say now that she was here in the witch's kitchen.

"I had nowhere else to go," Kelly finally admitted.

"I figured. I'm not one to refuse a guest who comes on open invitation. I told you to stay with me when you're in Sedona. You can stay as long as you're getting better. If you backslide or stall, you leave." Rattle sliced an extra-long ribbon of wood off the stick.

Kelly nodded.

"I'm not running some hippie detox retreat. You're not here to charge up your chakras by blinking your asshole at the sun. You go up the road to Penis Temple for that."

"There's a Penis Temple?"

Rattlesnake laughed. "Venus Temple, Penis Temple, whatever they call it. Don't actually go there though. It's a temple to worship money, not love or even sex. They built it on my ancestors' land, and they named it after an Italian lady. They'll rob you blind and shove pretty rocks up your cooch and call that a soul awakening. Know what I call that? I call it a pretty rock up your cooch. Helps with your Kegels, and that's about it."

Kelly laughed for the first time in weeks. Rattlesnake went on, "I fix people who need to be repaired, but only if they want it. I would've known immediately if you didn't really want it. Or if you didn't need it. You knew you needed my medicine. That's why you came here."

Kelly still had a long way to go in learning her own magic. She was pretty sure it didn't come from her mother's side, the German side, though Critter had some aptitude with hoodoo; maybe Critter's dad had the blood. No, the magic must've come through her father's line, the blood he wouldn't discuss. He said he was an orphan of the Korean War. Perhaps it was true. But Kelly could feel that there were grandmothers and great-grandmothers, aunties and even a few uncles, talking to her in her blood.

"Which side did you get your magic from, Rattle?"

Rattlesnake grimaced. "From both sides. I was marked from birth. My daddy's daddy was a skinwalker. A mean old coyote bastard, but he loved his family. Never saw him eat anyone he actually loved. My mother was dilbaa. Do you know what that is? She was never quite a man or a woman and didn't need to be. I guess I take after her, but I know some of Granddaddy's tricks. For one thing, I can smell evil, just like you can. Maybe we have blood in common."

"Do I smell like evil?"

Rattle flared their nostrils. "Yes and no. It's all over you, but it isn't a *part* of you. It's a crust you've gotta break and leave behind."

The image of the crust disgusted her. Like some kind of all-over scab or the dried-up honey look of a staph infection. Kelly shuddered. "Like I'm one giant wound, sparkling with lymph . . ."

Rattlesnake cackled. "So dramatic! If that's the image that gives you power, sure, but I can't see that being very good to dwell on. I was thinking more like a cocoon you gotta crack. You gotta dissolve into your ancient waters before you firm up into a new shape inside the shell. Then you bust out."

Ancient waters. Primordium. Ectoplasm. Kelly's mind flitted like a hummingbird from one thing to the next. These abstract terms for things so fundamental, so essential: it was hard to describe them in words. The terms smelled like dead crabs and rubies, and they coagulated into an image. Kelly envisioned Tiamat, the Mother Chaos whose lobster-dragon body was cracked apart, releasing reality—her corpse used to build all of the Something out of the primordial Nothing.

Or so she'd read.

"What are you making?" she asked, pointing to the woodwork in Rattle's hands.

"Not sure yet. It'll tell me what it wants to be."

"I think I need to sleep." She finished her cup of tea, and Rattlesnake made the couch into a bed for her. Rattlesnake kissed her lips and tucked her in. As Kelly slipped in and out of consciousness, she realized that her clairolfaction had returned with the brine-scented vision of Tiamat. She smiled and cried herself to sleep. It didn't take long.

She regained her strength. The withdrawal wasn't as horrific as she'd expected, but she was in the care of some big medicine. Her appetite and her bowels began to function normally again, and she could think in a straight line. Rattlesnake put her to work as an apprentice, sharpening her mind as well as her intuition. The two sat side by side, carving tools from the cottonwood that grew around

Rattle's property. Kelly learned to blend teas, to wildcraft paperflower and snakeweed, and she learned the powers of the sand. She made her own iris-violet emetic and felt like she would die after taking it.

"Something in you *is* dying. And good riddance," was all the comfort Rattle gave during the emetic ceremony. When Kelly's body was done purging, Rattle closed the ceremony and only then did they swaddle Kelly in blankets.

"Is this the worst part? Is the worst part over?" Kelly expected Rattlesnake to laugh at her, but they just held her and said, "That, my sweet, is entirely up to you."

Kelly felt hollow. Not like a soulless body—but like a musical instrument, a flute of bone that the breath of the Goddess could now flow through once again. Finally, the night after the emetic ceremony, Rattlesnake and Kelly made love. Her cup was clean and empty. She and Rattle set about filling it with the only things worth holding.

The next morning Kelly woke alone in Rattle's bed. The sounds and smells of frying filled the house. She took her time getting up.

She practically danced into the kitchen, right up to Rattlesnake, and gave them a fat kiss on the cheek. Rattle had put on a feast: eggs and hash, collard greens, fruit and yogurt, coffee and orange juice, and brown bread with jam and butter. The two of them ate and ate.

It was past noon when Kelly cleared the table. Rattle objected to her doing the dishes, but she insisted. The past weeks invigorated her. She felt weightless yet mighty, like Supergirl.

Rattle dried the dishes. When Kelly was almost done scrubbing, they said, "Hey, Kel. I got one more thing to give you. I don't think you're gonna like it."

She nearly dropped a plate. She wasn't weightless anymore.

They sat at the table. Rattlesnake took Kelly's hand. "You and me, we get on great. But I broke some rules with you. There are rules for witch people, Kelly. Rules for integrity. Damage control. I love having you here, but I can't let you stay much longer."

"But I like it here. I'm even starting to get used to the desert. I like being your apprentice and your lover—"

"And that's a problem, Kelly. I can't have both in one person. It's not a clean boundary. I don't wanna be that witch. I shouldn't have let you create a story in your head about a future here. It was selfish of me."

The tears spilled down Kelly's cheeks. "No. You don't really believe this. You're just pushing me away because you love being alone."

Rattlesnake looked her in the eye. They didn't need to say it. Kelly knew from the look on their face. All she smelled was the kitchen.

"Kel, I'm trying to apologize and make things right between us. You didn't even know I strayed from my path. Of course, I love being alone. I want to be. I'm meant to be. I knew you'd come find me one day, and I knew it wouldn't be until you were in some real trouble. That's your path. It leads here and then on. My path leads me to you and then on. I can't be your mentor *and* your lover *and* your healer. The power here is wrong, and I'm making it right."

Kelly got desperate. She felt like she was using again, fully helpless and dependent on something outside herself. "Please, Rattle. I'll die. I'll relapse and die if you kick me out now."

Rattle squeezed her hand. "No, that's not the story I'm weaving. You can weave your own, but I didn't spend weeks nursing you and teaching you just to throw you to the scorpions. I wanted you here. I wanted to help you. And now I need to let you help yourself. I can't keep you here, but I can give you something to keep you safe."

Kelly shook her head, knowing that absolutely nothing could change Rattle's mind once it was made up.

Rattle withdrew their hand and turned both palms up for Kelly to inspect. "You know some things about my kinfolk. Witch people shift. Some, like my grandaddy, can become something else—coyote, sage, even sand. Some, like my mama, can be man or woman or someone in between, like me. Put those two bloodlines together, you get some new kinds of witch people."

Like a lightning flash, a bone-white barb flicked out of the palm of each hand. What Kelly had taken for a freckle or a scar was revealed to be a tiny orifice, one on each palm, equipped with a retracted fang poised to unsheathe and bite at any moment. "I'm a snake witch. These are my fangs."

Taking care not to touch these new organs, Kelly turned Rattlesnake's hands over. The backs of the hands appeared as expected. "So you're venomous? There's poison in your hands?"

"Poison to some. Medicine to others. Most people get the latter. This is what I have for you if you want it. I can prick you with my left hand and cure your addiction for good. I can rewrite the story of your nervous system and make it so that you will never crave morphine or oxycontin or any other strain of opioid ever again. It will be repugnant to you. It's my biggest magic, and there's a price."

Of course there was a price. Kelly thought getting put outside of this perfect home was the price, but losing Rattlesnake was merely incidental. "It's not a devil's bargain, but it's sacred, and it hurts the way some sacred things do. The price for me is I lose you. That's what it costs me to heal you right and set you free. The price for you is up to the medicine. How much do you want to be free of your addiction?"

Kelly thought about all the time she'd lost. She wouldn't lose any more of her life to a pill or needle. She could smell truth again. She could hear the goddess talking again. What was that worth?

"Do it."

"Are you absolutely sure, Kelly? I can't undo it once it's done."

"Fucking do it before I change my fucking mind, Rattlesnake. I love you. Make me better."

Rattlesnake took a large gulp of their tea. "Aright. Take your pants off. It works best in the leg."

Kelly slipped off her pajama bottoms. She'd put on clean panties before leaving the bedroom. For this small comfort, she was grateful.

"Wait," Kelly said. Rattlesnake paused. "You said the medicine is in your left hand? What's in the right hand? The poison?"

"You do not want to know," was all Rattle would tell her.

Kelly sat and extended her leg. Rattle placed their hand on Kelly's pale thigh. She winced and recoiled even before the puncture came, but it was almost painless. Rattlesnake stood up and kissed her on the crown of her head. Kelly asked, "What happens now?"

"Now we wait it out. If it gets bad, I'll take care of you."

Kelly felt warmth spreading from the site of the bite. It felt good at first and then like anxiety in her leg instead of her chest or head. The leg started to tingle like it didn't have enough blood. She moaned, and Rattle asked her what she was feeling.

"Pins and needles, huh? That's not the worst thing that could happen. You may have neuropathy from the bite."

"Neuropathy? Like my leg is dying?"

"No, that's necropsy. I can feel your pulse in your thigh. The blood is flowing, so the leg isn't dying. You're not gonna have a zombie leg. You may need to walk with a cane from now on."

The medicine took its price. Kelly's leg had tingled, sometimes unbearably, ever since. Sometimes she regretted the bargain. Sometimes she regretted not taking it sooner.

Rattlesnake gave her the cane that they'd whittled and sanded with their own hands. "Now we know what it was for. Funny how the magic sets everything up for you, and you just gotta walk into it when it calls."

"The cane is magical? What does it do?"

Rattle cackled. "Goddamit, Kelly. It helps you walk is what it does. Cottonwood is sacred, but it's not gonna channel lightning or turn into a serpent if you tap it three times. If it does, you best call me."

Kelly giggled. "You never answer your phone."

"And you never call. You text. So text me now and then. I'm gonna miss you."

Kelly kept in touch with Rattle but hadn't seen them in person since leaving Arizona. Every year, on the "birthday" of the bite, Rattle sent her a care package full of home blended tea and occasionally a bumper sticker from the Venus Temple. The last one read, "Come and Be Healed," with a note in sharpie on the back in Rattle's handwriting: *Can you believe this shit?*

Soon, Kelly discovered there was another gift tucked into the medicine from Rattlesnake's bite: when she was in danger, the tingling vanished. The leg was still stiff and a challenge to walk on, but Kelly found she could rely on the tingle. If the leg pained her, she was safe.

Tuesday, January 7

The neuropathy sparkled in every step she took in the underground garage. Critter offered an elbow to her, but she refused. The two of them walked with Julian toward the detective's car.

It had taken most of the evening to iron out their plan and gather materials. Some charms had to be brought in by air courier. Even so, they agreed it was better to invest the time into preparing rather than race an arbitrary clock. They decided to get a little rest if they could and set out before dawn.

"We should assume he knows we're coming," Sophia said before they left her office. She withdrew a handgun from her jacket pocket, as if to emphasize the danger, and slid it out of sight again.

"How useful are guns in this situation?" Kelly wondered aloud. "Like, don't bring a knife to a gun fight? Don't bring a gun to a wizard's duel."

"Worked fine last time," Aweke mumbled.

"This Leng is not a golem. He'll have different strengths. Aim for the heart," Martinetti quipped. "If you can't hit the heart, aim for the solar plexus or his crotch. We want to hit a chakra center if we can. Punch a hole in his aura so his magic leaks out."

Critter pulled a sachet from his pocket. "Um . . . I don't think I'm . . . prepared."

Martinetti raised one eyebrow. "Would you like to stay here?"

Critter looked at his shoes.

"Here," Aweke handed him a small gun with a translucent white barrel. "The bullets are selenite. It's pretty useless except at close range. Never aim it at another person unless you are trying to kill them. Hold the gun in both hands, away from the body. None of this gangster stuff holding it above your head and pointing it down at someone. You'll break your wrist when it kicks back. Never, ever aim it at yourself or someone on your side. Do you understand?"

Critter got excited and examined the pistol. "You said selenite? So is this, like, blessed by Selene?"

Aweke fumed. "I will take that gun right back from you, and you can sit in the car."

"Enough," Martinetti almost whined. "Julian, he gets it. Critter, yes, it's sacred to whatever moony goddess you want it to be. Hecate, Lilith, Chang Xi. Just don't shoot your balls off, and don't shoot any of us."

Critter was silent for a moment. "I don't have balls," he reminded Sophia.

"Oh," Martinetti said. "Right. You know what I mean."

"What are you packing, Sophia?" Kelly scanned the other woman: handgun holstered to her middle; gold neck chain, presumably with an amulet dangling at its nadir; one boot slightly asymmetrical to the other for sheathing a knife or a wand or maybe even a syringe.

"I see you undressing me with your eyes, Kelly." If this was a joke, Kelly wasn't in the mood. She rolled her eyes, and so did Martinetti. "Gun and bullets with a homing spell. They'll hit the target unless the target's protections are stronger than my magic. I've got a fat fire agate over my heart and a silver knife in my boot."

That, plus Kelly's tools, would have to suffice.

Down in the garage, Kelly eased herself into the backseat, and only then did Critter come around to the other side and get in. Julian was already warming up the car.

As soon as Kelly pulled her door shut, the tingling in her leg stopped.

"Put up your protections," she told the others. The detective put a hand to his gun, as if that was any protection at all. Critter pulled a small velvet bag out of his pocket and clutched it to his stomach. Kelly breathed into her deepest place, concentrating on a sense of perfect safety. The tingle returned, though faintly.

"He's trying something, but we should be okay as long as I'm tingling."

Critter exhaled in relief. Aweke grunted and pulled the car out from its parking space. Slowly, the vehicle made its way along the concrete spiral, up and up, closer to the surface. They left the garage without any issues or surprises.

Kelly could track Martinetti's car a hundred or so feet ahead of them, a flashy little Italian thing made by a company Kelly had never heard of.

"Is Sophia driving herself?" Critter asked. "She doesn't seem like the type."

"No. She has a self-driving car," Aweke said. "She calls it her 'auto-auto.' God knows how much she spent on it."

"Probably nothing," Critter said. "She seems awfully good at getting what she wants."

Julian changed lanes. "I don't like the implication."

"I didn't realize I made one. Did I?"

"*Boys*," Kelly barked. "I'm trying to concentrate on protecting us."

The neuropathy was still faint, but it was there. It wasn't a calibrated tool though. It was just her leg. Kelly had no idea whether the faintness meant they were out of mortal danger or still kind-of-sort-of in it. Martinetti's car avoided bridges and alleys, places where the cars would be more open to an attack. Detective Aweke followed Martinetti like he was following an order.

Finally, they came to a gravel parking lot near Lumen Field and parked. The rocks beneath them, which would've been wet and gray after any other rain, were still slick with the blood that had fallen from the sky yesterday.

She saw Sophia tromping across the bloody gravel, the wet rocks grinding like teeth beneath her boots. She hoped Martinetti had enough self-control to follow the plan. Kelly got out of the car and followed with the men in tow.

In a few blocks, they reached the old INS building. The windows were dark, and the decrepit sodium streetlamps gave it all a yellow tinge. From the front, it didn't look like a jail. It looked like a school, and it was easy to imagine it as an assay station during the gold rush. It smelled like gold, now that Kelly was within a hundred feet of it. Gold and human misery, like the Vatican smelled when she visited it once. The Vatican, however, had a comforting scent of balsam incense and ripe hope blanketing everything else. She'd never smelled anything that mixed joy and misery in such a powerful mélange. Bells and smells.

Kelly stared at the building. "We can't just go in guns a-blazin'. There could be civilians in there. Most of them probably have no idea who Abraham Leng is."

"You said his lab was under the building, intersecting the hell realm." Aweke fingered the gun concealed in his suit.

"I mean, yes and . . ."

"And what?" Aweke looked impatient. Kelly figured it was his way to avoid looking frightened. "I don't want to harrow any hell realms today. I just want to take out Leng, once and for all, on the most stable ground possible. Can we stay on this side of that intersection? The not-hell side?"

Kelly drew in a deep breath. She was able to concentrate enough to pick out the nuances in her clairolfaction. Top notes: the physical scent of Chinatown; the trees and the street; the hot meats and the steamed vegetables; dim sum and car exhaust. Mid notes: the psychic impressions of the neighborhood; a scent of old books and discontinued cosmetics; the talcumed skin of elder relatives; betelnuts and champa; cool ginkgo trees and hot neon. Alongside that were the fat notes of gold and suffering that the INS building represented.

The base note was—what? Something so faint yet absolutely there. Another cloaking spell. All she could get was the impression of sweet, fresh water surrounded by a salty sea.

Kelly suddenly doubled over. She retched, and a fountain of seawater cascaded out of her mouth. The others took a step back. Kelly felt it shoot out of her ass as well, her body expelling it as quickly and efficiently as it could.

Critter came to her then, squatting beside her, taking her hand and holding her hair back from her face. She tried to speak, but more brine poured out. It was pure and cold, no sign of food matter in it. The salinity burned her rectum, but that too seemed to be clear and devoid of fecal matter. Thank the Goddess for small favors.

One more heaving retch brought up the largest draught yet, and then the cramps subsided. Kelly spat and blew her nose. Her leg tingled, giving her its ironic sense of safety.

"Is she okay? What was that?" The detective tapped the brine puddle with the toe of his boot.

Kelly wasn't ready to talk, and Critter seized the opportunity. "That was the final cloaking spell breaking," he said. "I think."

Kelly breathed in through her nose and out through her mouth. The scent of bardo nearly knocked her on her ass. It was indescribable in purely fragrant terms. It was *like* the scent of electricity arcing through steam inside a copper tank. It was *like* the scent of Doctor Frankenstein's laboratory, raw story and pure creative potential, all channeled through an idea—an imagined simulacrum of impossible science. It smelled like alchemy and hubris.

This was the bardo scent clinging to city for the last week. It poured out of every steam vent, cloaked in water vapor. It leaked from the taps in kitchens and bathrooms. It tainted every drop of rain. And it all came from this building.

As long as her leg prickled, she could trust that she was safe. One breath at a time. Kelly spat once more, stood up tall in her cold, wet jeans, and walked straight into the lobby of the Inscape building.

Critter followed closest. He pulled out a hagstone—an authentic one, its holes bored by the Orkney channels and whatever stone-eating worms and mollusks dwelt there. He had the stone up to his eye before he even crossed the threshold.

"See anything?" Kelly asked as Martinetti and Aweke entered behind them.

"Gimme a sec! It's a hagstone not a telescope." Critter scanned the room. Kelly didn't see, hear, or smell anyone else in the lobby. If there were artists in here, they were absorbed in the act of creation, like little bees working on their own little pockets of honeycomb.

Critter completed a full 360-degree turn with the stone to his eye. "Hm. Nothing. Are you sure that the last cloaking spell is broken?"

Kelly experienced a sudden wave of dizziness and disorientation. For a moment, she felt like she would fall through the ceiling. She swayed, and her cane gave way, but Aweke caught her elbow and steadied her.

"Easy, Mun. What are you getting?" He put a strong but gentle hand on her back.

"We're right on top of it. There's nothing above ground but interference. We have to make our way down."

"Ho . . . lee . . . balls . . ." Critter said. He was staring through the stone at the floor.

"What? What do you see?" Julian snatched the stone from him and looked through. "The floor is . . . lava? Oh, give me a fucking break."

He handed it to Kelly. Critter said, "The whole floor is alive. Like smooth pink muscle tissue, pulsing and constantly swallowing energy."

Kelly didn't see lava or flesh through the stone tool. She saw a blood-red whirlpool filling the entire floor, even the adjoining hallways. The maelstrom pulled spectral blood, like veins through the halls and down into the mouth of the eddy, which happened to be centered in the spot where Kelly had just been standing.

There was something else. Gaseous gray forms hovered in the air beside, above, and sometimes even through the four investigators. The amorphous masses looked like wisps of steam, but they weren't steam.

"Ghosts," she told the others. "We're shin-deep in an energy sink. One so strong that it sucks the ghosts right out of the air. I don't know if it consumes them like fuel or sends them to a hell realm or turns them into bardo, but it's drinking the psychic energy of all the people who lived and died here."

"And you want us to follow this rabid rabbit hole down to hell?" Aweke had his palm to his forehead.

Kelly shoved him with an open hand. "You wanna stay behind? Do it. Cover us. We'll call you for back up if we can use you."

She glared at Martinetti, who glared back. Julian broke their staring contest and asked, "What do you want me to do?"

Sophia said nothing, just looked to Kelly. Kelly said, "I do think you'll be of the most help if you stay here and keep anyone—or thing—from following us down. Critter, you stay with him."

"But I'm your partner!" he protested.

"You're safer up here with Detective Aweke. And Julian is safer with you. The two of you can protect each other better than you can protect me and Sophia. Stay here, Critter. Please. Protect Julian with your tools and let him protect you. He's a professional. Trust him. And Julian—do not let anything happen to my baby cousin, you hear me?"

Julian nodded with that mortal seriousness that cops so often showed. He did not protest. Critter blushed and looked down.

Kelly and Sophia looked at one another, neither moving to take the lead. "You first, boss," Kelly finally said.

Martinetti narrowed her eyes and went in the direction of the stairwell.

"Do you need the hagstone?" Critter called after them.

"Keep it. Use in good health," Kelly called back. Martinetti scowled at her.

"If I wasn't positive that he knows we're here," Kelly said, "I wouldn't be this loud."

That seemed to satisfy Sophia, uncharacteristically quiet as she'd been since they got here.

"All business," Kelly said. "In and out. Break the binding spells on the goddesses, free the human captives. Take out the warlock—permanently. Avoid civilian casualties at all costs."

At the basement level, they emerged from the stairwell.

The hall was dim but not dark. A bit of yellow-tinted light came in from high windows at ground level. The main hall seemed deserted. Doors lined the cold and cluttered space. Finished and unfinished art projects leaned against the walls here and there along with the bric-a-brac one would expect in a communal basement.

Kelly crouched—the pain in her leg was still faint but present—and pulled a sachet from her jacket. Sophia pulled out her gun, and Kelly was dumbstruck to see that it was an actual Gucci glock. Kelly's body language gave away her disdain, and Martinetti just shrugged.

Kelly refocused on the tools at hand. She took out a little handful of dust and blew it into the air in front of them. A few motes caught the light. "Grave dirt. New Orleans Cemetery Number One. Purest shit money can buy." She didn't know if she explained it for her own confidence or Sophia's.

Kelly removed a darkly rusted railroad spike from the same pocket. "Our great great grandmother drove this spike herself, so the story goes. Critter did the research. She posed as a man and worked building the rails. We found the exact stretch she'd worked on and dowsed the shit out of it last year." Then she declared, "Show yourselves," and drove the spike against the cold concrete floor.

The space around them flickered like a heat mirage, and the gray spirit forms appeared again. The energy sink still drew them downward, spiraling toward the center of a blank wall a few yards ahead. "There's the soft place," Kelly said. "I mean, obvi."

She inhaled, despite the grave dust dancing in the air. "But Leng is over there." She pointed toward a doorway opposite the epicenter. As though on cue, the stained glass in the door lit up.

"Fuck," Kelly said. "We are really doing this." Sophia stayed silent. Kelly kind of missed her shady comments.

They walked sideways, back-to-back, down the hallway. The gray souls still moved through the space, but no demons or monsters revealed themselves. So far, no traps.

The door with the stained glass had a sign on it in a sinuous Art Nouveau script: *Madame Lulu,* and underneath that, *Psychic, Tarot, Palm Reading.*

"Great cover, isn't it? A power-crazed alchemist hiding out as a carnival-variety huckster. Gotta give him credit for audacity."

On the opposite wall, the misty soul-forms continued spiraling into the soft place. Two black painted handprints haunted that wall along with a plaque explaining that this is where INS prisoners were forced to spread their legs and lean against the wall for body searches. It was the softest place in the building, and it smelled overpoweringly of fear.

"On the other side of those handprints is where the goddesses are being held. 'Madame Lulu's office' is where Leng and our human friends are. Now, don't do anything too rash."

Gun pointed straight ahead of her, Sophia Martinetti turned the knob and opened the illuminated door.

"Found me!" The chipper voice announced.

Martinetti fired immediately. Her bullet stopped six inches from her target's chest and fell to the floor. Kelly sighed in frustration.

A slender, middle-aged man in a crisp brown suit leaned back against a desk. The room was more spacious than expected, though not enough to defy the laws of physics. It was an office and firmly grounded on the earthly plain. In one corner, naked, bound by zip ties and gagged, were Harriet, Ben, and Tonya.

Dr. Leng smiled, slapped his thigh, and said, "You had to try, right? It could've worked if you knew what you were doing, Sophie."

"Jesus, how well do you two know each other?" Kelly asked.

Leng hissed. "She was an employee. A lieutenant at best. Tried to convince me to make her an apprentice."

"And you didn't tell me?" Kelly kept her eyes on Leng, but Martinetti's secrets were becoming a liability and a distraction.

"Alright, you insufferable cunts." Leng stood up. "Now that you're finally here, follow me. Or I'll start killing your friends."

Ben and Tonya blinked through tears. Harriet's eyes blazed with rage.

Kelly's leg stopped tingling, and she could put her full weight on it. She and Sophia followed Dr. Leng to the soft place.

SEVERAL HORRIBLE WAYS TO DIE

S HE EXPECTED IT TO MAKE A SOUND. WHEN SOMEONE CROSSED A PORTAL in a movie, it made a sound like a *whoosh* or a *bloop* or an electric crackle. As they passed through the soft place, it didn't sound like anything. That was good.

At Leng's insistence, Martinetti went first. That was also good. It would buy her a few seconds to do what she needed to do on the other side. Kelly hesitated and then went through next. Leng took a while to follow through, at least on the other side of the veil. Who knew how time worked when crossing into a hell dimension.

"Please, take it in," he told them as he arrived. "We have plenty to see."

The cavern looked perfectly subterranean with its stone floor and stalagmites. It was cold rather than hot—the very nadir of a Dantean or Buddhist hell. There was no sky nor roof visible, just a dark abyss above them, but there were walls. Walls of glass, some thick and opaque, others thin and clear and brittle, met at strange angles in a broken labyrinth. The angles seemed as random as shattered glass, like a German expressionist skyline. Glass shards mingled with ice crystals in ways difficult to discern one from another. Some of the walls were mirrors, like the wall they'd just passed through.

This was not a soft place; this was a hard, sharp, frozen place.

A gentle contrast of blue-white light came from the floor and the walls, provided by pale glowworms or maggots or some other wretched form of demonic life. Martinetti pressed in close to Kelly. The warmth of her body was a tiny comfort, but Sophia stank of fear. Kelly had never smelled that much fear on Sophia before, but considering the circumstances, it was no surprise.

More crystals, neither glass nor ice but more like quartz and gypsum, grew here and there in fractal anemones. As far as actual plant or fungal life, lichens were all Kelly noticed. It grew on the walls and on skewers of huge, splintered bones that stuck up from the floor at random angles. They could've been the bones of giants or dragons. Maybe they grew organically from the floor itself.

"Which hell is this?" Kelly asked, her breath visible.

Leng snickered. "Truly, I don't know. It told me it wants to be called Gelis Kaca, which means something like 'cold shard of glass' or 'sharp ice crystal.'"

"It's sentient? The realm talks to you?"

Leng sneered. "Yes, dingbat. Of course it does. Gelis Kaca is a petite hell from a forgotten cult. Or maybe it was created right here from the agony of the detainees. Prime real estate if you ask me. The locals weren't really doing anything with it."

He plucked a pale blue maggot from the wall and crushed it between his fingers. Then he ate it. He sucked his glowing fingertips and said, "They're delicious, and they give you the ability to smell fear."

"I can already smell fear," Kelly told him. "The whole place is nauseous with that smell."

Leng frowned and said, "Well, good for you, candy ass. I'm sure that comes in handy in your line of drudgery."

She had expected Leng to be a stone-faced psychopath, an intimidating gangster who spoke quietly and carried several big guns. The man throwing sass at her was almost cartoonish—deceptively so. His pencil mustache and brown pinstripe suit looked more like an old comic-book villain than an ice-cold murderer. He reminded her of El Catrin, the Dandy, from the loteria cartomancy deck. If his mustache were thicker, he might've twirled it. The picture of Leng she held in her head up to now was Al Capone mixed with Ted Bundy, that kind of easy, deadpan evil. She had not expected Leng to look more like Cab Calloway and talk like Vincent Price, gleefully planning to flay her with a twinkle in his eye.

"Stay on this side of the labyrinth," Leng told them. "Its sole purpose is to confuse you, stab and cut you, until it strips you of all hope. That's not *my* plan for you though. Come, see the merchandise for yourselves." He gestured for them to follow a corridor that ran along one stone wall of the cavern. "It's just up ahead on the left."

Sure enough, a branching tunnel opened in the stone wall, leading away from the mosaic of jagged crystals. The length of it, about twenty yards, glowed blood red. The light here shone brighter than the blue light of the glow-maggots in the labyrinth, but it was still as dim as twilight. Whatever it was at the end of the tunnel, it wasn't fire, though it might've been red-hot.

The closer they came to this chamber, the more movement Kelly noticed. A flicker at first, then blobs of shadow. The light threw a strange collage of shapes onto the walls, some of them lifelike, some monstrously mechanical. Leng had called whatever he kept in here "merchandise," and Kelly clenched her jaw at that. She knew what she'd find there, but she hoped with desperation that it would be anything else.

The eeriest part was that no noise came from the room at the end of the tunnel. The three of them walked, and their footsteps made soft noises on the floor of this passage, but no sound came from the red room.

When they were almost to the end, Leng began to bloviate again. "What you *aren't* hearing is a sound-cloaking spell. It took me days to get it just right. The bardo farm is very noisy. It was distracting. But here we go. Check this out!"

He led them into the bardo farm.

There were so many. About a dozen and a half, Kelly estimated—so many more than she and the others had identified from the overdose victims. A few feet from her, spitting and snarling inside an iron cage, was the living severed head of a dark-skinned woman. That was probably Ti Kitha Demembre. Kelly didn't see the rest of her divided body.

Over there was Ixtab, the Hanged Goddess, caught in the web of chains Kelly had seen in her vision of this place. A few feet beyond that, a distinctly female thing struggled, naked and emaciated, on the metal rack that restrained her. Her antlers cracked as she lashed them back and forth, little chips of them flying here and there. Maybe Leng would try to sell those too, grinding them into a powder for snorting.

In a glass vat, Shub-Niggurath slammed herself against the transparent walls. She beat them with her split hooves and raked them with her spidery palps and claws. Her eight human breasts flattened when she mashed the front of her body against the glass.

And there were others. Too many others. One looked like a flower in the shape of a woman, a weeping eye in the center of her whorl of petals. Eostre? Another woman sat restrained in a chair, some gruesome apparatus holding her jaws wide apart. Kelly saw that her cheeks were torn. That was probably the Kuchisake Onna.

One spirit even seemed trapped in a mirror, her blood washing down the flat glass into runnels beneath. That had to be Bloody Mary or some other iteration of the urban legend. Her blood glowed, one source of the red light in the room. All their blood glowed. It was bardo.

Each spirit seemed caught in some mess of metal, chain, glass, and wire—and each one bled. Brassy tubes pumped their blood right out of their bodies, or else collected it as it dripped. Everywhere she looked, there were women in pain, their very blood harvested like they were animals. It was a factory farm, plain and simple—but these chattels were immortal. Kelly saw them tremble and thrash and scream in anger and despair, but the room remained silent.

She scanned for Brigid but couldn't pick her out from the other prisoners. She couldn't hear her special goddess's voice inside her, but she felt her presence. Where was Leng keeping her?

She tried to speak, but no sound came.

"Oh, you can't make sounds in here," Leng told her. "Only I can. It's the nature of the cloak."

This fucking guy, Kelly thought. Kelly hoped Sophia could somehow read her mind. *Don't do anything stupid, Sophia. Stick to the plan.* She twisted the thought up into a projectile and flung it at Martinetti.

"This is what I'm most proud of," Leng said with a tear in his eye. "This is the new peak of the pyramid. Drugs and guns led me to alchemy, and alchemy led me to all of this. These cows bleed magic and money, and they never run out."

He clapped his hands once in the soundless cave, making Kelly and Sophia both jump. "So I'm not one for big Hollywood villain speeches—"

Liar, Kelly thought.

"—but I'm sure you two wondered, 'Why are they all female?' A pertinent question. Male gods and spirits are definitely more common, but they're usually stronger. They have bigger cults and more pervasive superstitions. I needed to start with the weaker sex. All these ladies have their believers but not too many.

And they're all a few steps removed from actual gods. That Voodoo one, for instance, she's not even a real loa. And the spider-goat-whatever-she-is . . . I have no idea where she comes from. I think she's from a comic book or something. I wouldn't try to capture a big goddess like Venus or Pele. Not yet.

"I'll move onto male spirits soon enough. I can't grab a Santa Claus or a Cupid until I scale way up. Maybe a second-rate superhero or two, or some minor saints. Saint Sebastian obviously. Have to learn to crawl before you learn to walk."

Much was still hidden, cloaked in lies and half-truths. He had Brigid stashed somewhere, and she was both a saint and a goddess. He had enough power to bind her, but where?

"Any questions?" Leng cocked his head. Sophia opened her mouth, but no sound came. "Just kidding! Let's go somewhere we can actually talk."

The trio walked back through the tunnel and into the hell of ice and glass.

"You are every bit the monster that I've heard," Kelly said when she had her voice back.

"Thanks," Leng said. "I keep a low profile, but I love to leave an impression. For the record, I'm impressed as well. Let's do some business."

He pulled what looked like an icicle from his jacket and blew through it, producing a piping note that sounded like pure despair. Three chairs of ice and a table of crystal formed from the ground up. The occultists took their seats.

"You've made it this far, and your magic is strong, but mine is stronger. A lot stronger." He placed the ice flute on the table. "I've also outwitted you at every turn."

Kelly looked to Sophia, who held her nose in the air and withheld comment. "Oh, you know I have," Leng continued. "You thought I was dead for the last year. It took you forever to figure out what was going on, and even then, you needed a private detective with a psychic nose to help you do it. No offense, Miss Mun."

She was about to say, "None taken," but the warlock kept on talking.

"This can go one of two ways." Leng was finally getting to the point. He waved his left hand as though conducting an orchestra. "Either I'll kill your friends in front of you before I bind you in a hell realm, or"—he made a similar motion with his other hand—"you can come work for me. You're more valuable to me alive and in my employ than dead and stubborn."

Kelly looked at Sophia. "He sounds exactly like you."

"I am *right here*, for fuck's sake," Leng said.

Kelly chuckled. "Now he sounds like Critter!"

Sophia smiled too, just enough to show some emotion. Kelly concentrated her thoughts on the Margaret Atwood quote, *Men are afraid women will laugh at them. Women are afraid men will murder them.* It became a mantra in her mind, strengthening her resolve and quelling her fear. Mess with his ego until he makes a mistake.

Leng's eyes began to glow as blue as the maggots on the walls. "Last chance, Kelly Mun. Come work for me and have a good life. Or spend eternity freezing and slicing off strips of your pretty skin in this gulag."

Kelly looked into those glowing eyes. "Where's the hook in the bait? It can't be that simple."

Leng smiled. "Of course it's not. I'll let your friends go, but Sophia dies."

He picked up the icicle pipe and jammed it through Martinetti's throat. "La belle dame sans merci," he said and pushed the still-gagging Martinetti off her seat and onto the frozen ground. "Au revoir."

His eyes ceased to glow. Kelly swallowed hard. That could've just as easily been her.

"So, Kelly. Let's talk business. I know you're not a fool. Now she"—Leng pointed his thumb at the body as it kicked out its death twitches—"was arrogant. Couldn't see what was right in front of her, even with her small army of underlings."

Kelly kept breathing steadily, kept her mind on the task at hand. "You drive a hard bargain, but of course, that's the point. Okay. I'll play along. What happens now?"

"Now," he said with all the treacle of a grandfather admonishing a child, "you tell me what you're hiding."

Would he call her bluff? They both knew she couldn't match his magic. A physical brawl would likely fail after what he'd done to that bullet Martinetti fired in his office, and he didn't need magic or much physical strength to send that ice pipe through her neck.

It was Kelly's wits he wanted to test. She met his challenge.

"I could ask you to tell me the same thing, Abraham. But neither of us is the kind to play all our cards in a single round. What answer could I possibly give you that would be satisfactory? Do I play the feint within the feint? 'Which door would the other guy tell me is the safe door.' I'm not sure what you're really asking me."

He knows this game, Kelly told herself. *Don't play him like a simple maniac. Stay unpredictable.*

"So the game is afoot, ey?" Leng sat back in his ice chair.

Kelly cocked an eyebrow. She continued mixing deceit with the bluntest truths. "The game was afoot days ago, Leng. I'm here on your turf, at your mercy. Please don't play coy."

Leng sighed. "Martinetti was so fun to tease. But you've got no taste for intrigue. You just want to slice through my intricate knots instead of unraveling them. Very well. Tell me everything you think you know about the project."

"That works. And you let me know if I've got it right or not. How about that?"

Leng gestured her to go ahead.

"Firstly, I don't think you're trying to market bardo. You're testing it out on the street but not to see how well it sells."

He sneered. "Not bad. So what do you think I'm actually up to?"

"You're testing it until you find a safer formula because you plan to take it yourself."

"God damn, Kelly Mun!" He applauded. "You really are good at this! Come and work for me, please? I would hate to kill a woman of your skill."

She started to feel her connection to Brigid again. It seemed like the more she called Leng out on his motives, the closer Brigid came to the surface of the cloaking spell he'd hidden her under.

Kelly kept going. "When you showed me your 'farm,' as you call it, I wondered at first why you needed so many goddesses if you're just harvesting their blood for yourself. But of course, it's the variety. You're an alchemist at heart. Trial and error. Controls and variables. And what really tickles you is the research. The sadism is just sauce to the goose. Your goal isn't the capture and torture of a handful of lesser goddesses, though I think you do enjoy it. Your bigger kick is the satisfaction of your curiosity. You're not a Capone. You're a Mengele."

Leng was uncharacteristically quiet at that. Kelly had a moment of panic that she'd said the wrong thing, enraging him, snuffing out his fascination with her instead of inflaming it. But thank all the goddesses, her leg tingled.

"Anyone can bind a demon, Kelly. That thing I sent after you, the one with the darling little swarm of vertebrae, that was nothing. Cannon fodder. It takes a special finesse and audacity to ensnare a god."

She let him keep talking. *He's just another client,* she told herself. *Just a paycheck. Let him blather on and charge him by the hour.*

Leng stood and launched into his next monologue. "If you aren't born a god, created from dream stuff and star fire, you have some options." He began to pace. Kelly kept sharp in case he was preparing to sucker punch her with an oblique spell or a quick shiv. "You can seduce a godhead, like Ganymede did, until he can't go on without you. Then he'll make you immortal. You get a constellation and a lifetime supply of life."

He stepped over the bled-out body of Martinetti. The blood was getting thick and dark in the cold. "I tried that route, but I was never very good at fucking. And I'm getting older, Kelly. The gods want youth and beauty. They want spark."

Where is he going with this? Kelly wondered. He rested his hands on the back of Sophia's ice chair but then lifted them with a slight gasp after a few seconds. So he was susceptible to the cold unless that was a performance.

"Another option is vampirism. Suck the vitality and magic right out of people via their breath, their blood, their semen. And then there's alchemy. Crack the secret of life. Become your own homunculus. Turn yourself from lead into gold, from meat and shit into diamonds. But vampirism isn't sustainable—you have to keep sucking once you start. And alchemy is, at best, a less than exact science."

Finally, the clincher. Kelly kept her spine rigid.

He walked around the table and stood behind her. She let him see her real fear, let him feel dominant. Her neuropathy was very faint now, but it was still there.

"So I decided to mix all three options. Suck the blood from the gods themselves and use alchemy to do it." He put his hands on her shoulders, and she flinched. "I don't hate women, you know. It's just that female spirits were the path of least resistance. Magic doesn't care about political correctness."

She could feel Brigid so close. Where in this hell was she?

"But I can't seem to get the dosage quite right. The balance of solvé to coagula eludes me. Bardo doesn't boil or freeze. It doesn't evaporate or crystallize. I've diluted it like a homeopath into one part per million, per billion, orders of magnitude, and I cannot get it to calm down enough to be nonlethal. That's why I need you. You tasted the bardo and survived unscathed."

So he knew about that. Of course he did. He brought his mouth to her ear, but the pins and needles in her leg grew sharper. She suspected he had Brigid in the one place no one was looking for a goddess.

"All you have to do is give me what I want. I want immortality. There is nothing else in this life worth killing for. Help me figure out the key to bardo."

Typical, she thought. The most powerful men in the world only cared about stiff dicks and immortality.

His fingers slid like a lover's along her neck. "Do it . . . or I'll slit your throat."

She shivered, but she kept her courage. "I expected nothing less. Of course I'll work with you. You knew I would."

Leng straightened his back and patted her shoulder. "Good girl." He walked back toward his original seat at the crystal table.

"But you must know by now that I'm just as stubborn and curious as you are. I have a thing or two I want you to let me in on."

He made a *tut tut* and sucked his teeth. He turned his back to her. "Get to the point, Kelly."

Oh, from you *of all people,* she thought, but she did as he asked. "I want to know where you're keeping Brigid."

He whirled on his heel and faced her. "Color me impressed yet again!"

"Your alchemy is strong enough to bind her, and she's no delicate hothouse flower. But she's the key, isn't she?"

Leng steepled his fingertips for his next big reveal. "Oh, I wish it were that simple, Kelly. Brigid should have been the perfect catalyst, the ultimate Philosopher's Stone, a bezoar of pure Prima Materia."

Now he was just enough off his guard. He was peacocking for her, but he mixed his terminology in a sloppy way. "A goddess turned saint, worshipped across time by papists and pagans alike. An alchemical kind of spirit. Mother of the waters, Lady of Imbolc, she who turns the glaciers into rivers."

"Leng. Please quit stalling. Where have you bound her?"

Leng frowned. "See, this is why you need me. You got so far, but you couldn't figure out which cabinet your little goddess is locked in. She's *inside* of me, you dumb bitch."

She had guessed correctly. Leng's arrogance would be his downfall.

It was then that Kelly's leg stopped tingling entirely. She was at her most vulnerable, and Leng at his own. It had to be—

"Now," Kelly said as calmly as she could.

In the span of a second, Sophia Martinetti uncloaked, grabbed the icicle flute from her golem's throat, and jammed it into Leng's heart. Kelly jumped up and sprayed him with the psychic mace as Sophia—the real Sophia—ducked out of the way. In the confusion, Kelly slipped the syringe from her coat, unsheathed the cap between her teeth, and jammed it into Leng's neck. The warlock roared at the women for surprising him, but the poison was already doing its secret work, and Brigid was leaking from his ribcage.

The goddess flowed out in pulses, graceful yet visceral. Soon, Leng bled from every orifice, and what he bled was Brigid. She trickled from his eyes and his ears, from his cock and his rectum and then from his nipples and pores and follicles. She draped herself across him like a shawl of blood.

Martinetti wiped the ice flute on Leng's blazer. "So. We caught the tiger. Now what do we do?"

"Stick to the plan," Kelly said. "Brigid and the venom should keep him occupied long enough. Grab a leg. And stay careful! He could be hemokinetic."

The two women dragged the warlock as the neurotoxin locked his muscles up and Brigid had her merry way with him. It was a clumsy journey.

"Come on, Sophia! I don't know how long this will slow him down."

Leng began to convulse.

"I'm fucking trying, okay? He's heavier than he looks." It was good to have Sophia back, but at least, the golem didn't talk.

Finally, they got Leng into the bardo farm.

It was utter cacophony in there. The silence cloak had broken, and there were signs everywhere that Leng's magic waned. Bloody Mary put cracks in her mirror prison. Ti Kitha Demembre chewed her way through the cage that held her head.

"We can't stay, Sophia. When the goddesses escape—and they will—we have to be gone."

Right on cue, Shub-Niggurath shattered her tank. The amniotic soup in which she'd been suspended washed across the floor, and it hissed where it touched the other infernal devices that held the goddesses down. Now the contraptions dissolved quickly.

Solvé, Kelly thought. *Get out before coagula.*

"You don't belong here," decreed a horse-headed goddess as she shook off her reigns and spit out her bit. "Go."

She dropped Dr. Leng's leg and grabbed Sophia's hand. The two of them ran and ran until they found the mirror through which they'd entered this cold hell.

"Does it work in reverse? Do we need Leng?" Martinetti yelled. "Oh my god, I look terrible," she added, fussing with her hair.

Kelly pushed her through and jumped into the mirror.

☿

"I am so fucking angry with you for dragging me into this," Harriet said when she was finally unbound and ungagged. "Seriously. I'm going to put a binding on you and Critter so you never come near me again."

Kelly suppressed a smirk. "That's fair. Let's just get out of here before something worse happens."

Harriet cooled a bit. "Does someone have a coat I can borrow? Literally in my bikini here."

Tonya was in an oversized Supersonics hoodie and nothing else. "I was snatched out of my bathtub," she said, looking around for some pants. The office of Dr. Leng was a cluttered mess, but it did have an extra pinstripe suit. "Oh, I cannot get my ass into these," she said, dropping the fitted pants.

"Don't take anything from the office," Kelly told them all. "No clothes, no souvenirs. Goddess knows what sort of hexes and boobytraps Leng put in here."

Tonya pursed her lips and stripped off the hoodie. Sophia and Ben snuck a look at her bare skin. "What? He put this on me when he took me. I almost felt sorry for him. Supersonics fan and all. What's that called? Stockholm sickness? When you like your kidnapper for giving you little comforts?"

Harriet gave Tonya her bikini top. "If you wanna cover up anything," she said.

"No one has to go naked in January," Kelly said. She gave Tonya her coat. She motioned for Sophia to do the same.

"Oh. Right." Sophia took off her shell coat and folded it gently before passing it to Harriet. "Careful with that. It's angora."

Harriet refused the gift. "It's not going to fit. And who the fuck wears angora into battle?"

"Critter and Julian are upstairs," Kelly said. "Hopefully, we can get everyone some warm clothes that fit."

Ben, fully clothed, just nodded and went with the group.

"So what was on the other side of this, anyway?" Harriet asked, peering at the handprints that marked the soft place.

"Hell," Sophia said.

"Like . . . Christian hell?" Harriet cocked an eyebrow.

"Buddhist, I'd guess," Kelly said. "Lots of broken glass and ice. Maybe Chinese or Indonesian? Hard to tell, it was all chaos in there."

"Sounds like hell to me," Tonya said, shrinking back from the area.

"We should bind it shut," Harriet said.

Sophia surprised Kelly by saying, "No. This may be the only way in and out. There are spirits in there who've been bound, exploited, and trafficked. Tortured too. They need to be able to escape. I'd be shocked if Leng ever makes it out of there."

On cue, several spirits came through the invisible portal. The flower-headed goddess emerged through the soft place on growing vines, crept like ivy up the wall, and vanished. Shub-Niggurath and a few others followed. Kuchisake Onna emerged last, carrying two long shards of glass that looked like butcher knives. The glass was wet with blood. She turned toward Kelly, opened her slashed mouth, and wagged her tongue before melting into the floor.

Many of the spirits that Kelly had identified were still in there. Kelly found no pleasure in imagining the agony they wrought on Leng.

"Can we fucking leave *right now*?" Harriet asked.

The group made its way up the staircase to the ground floor.

"You okay, Ben?" Kelly said as the five of them climbed the stairwell. He shook his head and swallowed. Sophia looked suspiciously at him. Kelly told her to take the others up to Julian and Critter and get them to safety.

"Ben, I'm sorry to do this while you're traumatized, but I need to hear you talk. I need you to prove that you aren't a golem planted by Leng."

Ben just shook his head and began to cry.

"Ben, I know. I'm so sorry. But I have to hear you say something that lets me know it's really you."

Ben looked at her, almost through her. Kelly rooted herself for an attack.

Ben made little clicking noises and then in a quavering voice said, "Eat ginger and burdock. Your yang is too low." He collapsed sobbing into her arms. She held him for a moment and then walked him the rest of the way up the stairs.

Friday, January 10

The trio arrived at their destination. It began to rain—pure, fresh water—as they parked at the curb, and Kelly took it as a very good omen. She led Ben and Tonya up the sidewalk to the front door, and it opened as they approached, spilling light into the unusually wet desert night.

Kelly made the introductions. "Rattlesnake, I want you to meet Ben Wei and Tonya Williams. They are here for your medicine."

"You are welcome in my home," Rattle said, initiating the new ritual. "I just put the kettle on for tea."

Later, while Tonya and Ben slept, Rattlesnake and Kelly sipped a different blend of tea on the couch. Kelly told Rattle the whole story.

"Absolutely crazy. Sick-in-the-soul crazy," Rattle said of Abraham Leng. "I want you to know that I have never, ever, *ever* sent my medicine by a third-party courier, let alone what's in my right hand. But I couldn't say no to you. Not if you asked me to sever my hand at the wrist and overnight it to you in a lunchbox full of ice."

Kelly furrowed her brow. "Really? You'd go that far for me?"

Rattlesnake almost did a spit take with their tea. "Hell no, I wouldn't cut off my own hand for you. Not you, not anybody. But here I am, still doing things for you that I don't do for anyone."

Kelly snuggled up to them. "Do you want to . . . you and me?"

Rattlesnake kissed her forehead. "It's not the right time. Maybe someday. Today, I'm helping those two souls you brought to me. That Ben is in real bad shape, but I think I can handle him. Tonya is a mystery. She's got a lot going on that I can't figure out yet. I think she's a natural witch, like you. That's how you two survived taking the drug."

Kelly pondered that. The term finally felt like it fit. *Witch.*

Rattlesnake continued. "I heard her praying to that Tiki Toddy Mamba. Sounds like she's finding her magic for real."

"Ti Kitha Demembre," Kelly said. "It's Creole."

"Ain't nothing." Rattlesnake sipped their tea. "Made up colonial bullshit."

Kelly grimaced and said, "Doesn't matter. She's real now. The difference between folklore and fakelore is"—she hesitated—"is . . . I don't know. But it's a hair-thin line, whatever it is."

"The great mystery," Rattle said and blew on her teacup. "Changing skins."

Kelly sighed. Rattlesnake took a sip and said, "Aw, listen to me going on like some magic Hollywood Indian. I don't know shit about the secrets of the universe. Does anyone? Your Dr. Leng sure didn't. I just know how to help people. That's enough for one lifetime."

Before long, Kelly was asleep. When she awoke alone on the couch, she found that Rattle had covered her with a quilt.

Saturday, February 1

"We don't *have* to do this, you know," Critter said. He fed old files into the shredder.

"I know." As sparsely decorated as their little two-room office was, Kelly had avoided packing up as long as she could. They were still unpacking things that should've been thrown out. At least Martinetti hired movers for them.

"He could still be here," Critter reminded her. "In the soft place. Plotting his revenge."

Kelly took a deep breath and listened for Brigid. *I'll protect you both.* Her leg tingled in a new way, more tolerable, but it still ceased whenever she was in immediate danger. Kelly tested it now and then by stepping into Seattle traffic.

"Leng has been shredded into pork floss by now. Body and soul. If he's somehow alive and conscious, it's because they're not done with him."

Critter bit at a hangnail. "But did we have to move into the same building? Seems like inviting drama."

Kelly laughed and unwrapped a picture frame. It was a picture of her parents.

"Martinetti has put so many protection spells on this piece of land that I doubt she even remembers all of them. Conducting our business on top of Leng's epicenter is probably the safest place in the world to do it. If he tried to escape, we'd know immediately. And lest I remind you, Martinetti is letting us occupy the office rent-free."

"Yeah, well. I don't like having a boss who buys a building on top of a literal hell and then tells us to move into it."

"She's not the boss. *I'm* the boss. She's just a wealthy client and patron."

"She made you an offer you couldn't refuse. Sounds like a boss to me. With Leng out of the way, is she, like, de facto Godmother of the Seattle Occult Mafia?"

"Not just Seattle. The whole West Coast—Anchorage to La Paz. So we best stay in her good books."

Critter rolled his eyes. "Ah. So we picked the devil we know. Delightful."

Kelly just laughed. "I'll handle Sophia. She's just another client. And she likes us. If she starts to be a danger, I'll smell it a mile away."

Yes. You will, Brigid told her.

Critter sat cross-legged on the floor with his laptop and ordered new furniture. "Nothing too showy, nothing in bad taste," he said, clicking Add To Cart on an area rug printed to look like a Ouija board. Kelly let him have his fun. Sophia was picking up the tab, after all.

"Whatever you want, sweetie, but remember—I get to choose my own desk and chair."

"I hope I'm not interrupting anything," Sophia said from the doorway.

Kelly didn't even look up from what she was doing. "Are you going to do this all the time now? Just drop right in?"

"Maybe. Long as you work under my roof." She strolled into the office, picked up a mug wrapped in newspaper, frowned, and set it back down. She grabbed a paper towel and wiped her hands.

Critter closed the laptop. "Thanks for the new furniture, by the way. That was above and beyond."

Martinetti dropped the crumpled paper towel into a waste basket. She walked to Critter and ruffled his hair. "Don't mention it. As long as you're on my payroll, I expect you to represent me. Your office is an investment in all our success. Speaking of which, there's something that needs your attention."

"Christburgers," Critter said and cleared his throat. "It's not you-know-who, is it?"

Kelly sniffed the air. "Nope, he's no threat. This is something more . . . atmospheric? It smells like . . . oh god. Sophia, why am I smelling old books and dead ants?"

Martinetti raised an eyebrow. "I'm hoping you can tell me." She extended two fingers on her left hand and drew a cross in the air, then a circle around it. All sounds from outside the room stopped. Even though she'd cast a sound-cloaking spell, she spoke in a quiet voice.

"Leng left a vacuum in the occult world. Silly me, I thought I could fill it before others noticed. But Leng disrupted things beyond our comprehension. He did some things that us mere humans aren't supposed to be able to do. The spirits and goddesses he captured were missing and in that hell realm long enough that something else tried to fill the void. Nature abhors a vacuum, but magic absolutely loves it. Something not quite human has gained a foothold in our world. Leng let it in, and it immediately started amassing power and followers. I want you to find it, assess the threat, and report back. Do not try to stop or contain it by yourselves."

Kelly and Critter gave one another a look. Kelly said, "Sending us into mortal danger again? Already?"

Martinetti shrugged one shoulder. "Don't pretend you didn't enjoy it."

"Fine, Sophia. What are the specifics?"

Martinetti smiled. "You two are going to love this. The divination team started picking up signs yesterday. It's a new cult of some kind. Not clear who or what they believe in, but whatever that thing is, it's in our world now. We don't know whether they created it or whether it came through from somewhere else. They're not very good at cloaking, but they're excellent at creating distractions. They thrive on secrets, information, and spectacle. They hide in plain sight, demanding attention as a way of diverting it from what they're really up to. And now they have a Necronomicon."

Critter's eyes nearly fell out of their sockets. "*The Necronomicon*?! Holy shit! It's not supposed to even be real. It's—"

"Fakelore," Kelly said. "Great. Another story wants to kill us."

Martinetti folded her arms and said, "No, no. There is no 'one true' *Necronomicon*. But there are grimoires out there that can be put into that category. What's a Necronomicon, after all? It's a book of dead names."

The color drained from Critter's face. If Martinetti noticed, she didn't care. "Someone's collecting dead names. Information is power, and you know how powerful names are."

Kelly saw Critter's entire demeanor change. She put an arm around him and asked Sophia, "Are they targeting trans people?"

Martinetti pursed her lips. Kelly noticed that she wore a different shade of lipstick than she did when they met a month ago. "We don't know. That would be a very interesting connection, considering. I think they're just amassing power right now for use later."

"Considering what?" Critter said, his color and chutzpah returning.

"Considering . . ." Martinetti teased out the moment, probably just to make him squirm. "Considering that all our current intel indicates that this isn't just any old cult, New Age or necromantic. It appears that the cult is made up entirely of drag queens."

Kelly's mouth dropped open. She hadn't smelled that coming.

Critter giggled. "Shut your dongsucker, Sophia. That's insane."

Sophia shrugged again. "Thought you'd like this case more than the last. So. What are a bunch of drag queens doing with a Necronomicon? Who is their charismatic leader? What is their god? The divination team says we have a few weeks, then the shit hits the fan. I'm counting on you two to find out whose shit and which fan. The clock is, quite literally, ticking. Any questions?"

Kelly shook her head. Critter was already typing and scouring the hexweb.

"Good," Sophia said, and she made a twist in her wrist and a finger snap that broke the cloaking spell. She walked out of their office.

"I'll make the coffee," Kelly said.

Outside the office door, Martinetti's staff were already hanging cedar and thuja branches over every doorway, window, and mirror.

"Do the computer and TV screens too," Critter yelled to them. "Can't be too cautious this time."

Kelly looked down into the black tank of the coffee maker. She couldn't see anything in the water. All she could smell was the old building and a tiny hint of danger. Her leg tingled.

Somewhere, deep in the nest of steam heating pipes, she thought she could hear an echo of Abraham Leng still screaming.

ACKNOWLEDGEMENTS

My greatest gratitude to my editor Scott Gable. Big thanks as well to all the blurbers: Annie, Susan, Eileen, Nick, Toby, and Ann. To my beta readers, Matt and Laura (김효진). Thanks as well to Tara and Desiree for being my publicity team, and to Levi for introducing me to them.

Sending love to my family, my partner Matt, and his family that has become mine. Matt, you make so much more possible in my life. Thanks as well to my Clarion West family, especially to my 2015 classmates and to our mentors. Y'all encourage me to be as weird as I am and to be good at it.

I thank the teachers who taught me how to read and write and the mentors in college and beyond who taught me how to write with sharp, gemlike fire.

And the dead. My dear ones who passed during the writing of this book: Mom, Dorian, Aunt Robin, Uncle Don. You are all sorely missed.

And in the end, like a coven priestess who has just lit the pyre beneath her inquisitors and colonizers, I thank the Goddess.

§

Evan J. Peterson was brought to life in Miami, Florida. He's an author and game writer whose works include *Drag Star!* (Choice of Games), the world's first drag performer RPG, as well as the books *The PrEP Diaries* and *METAFLESH* and the game *The Road to Innsmouth: Arkham Horror*. His writing has appeared in *Weird Tales*, *PseudoPod*, *Queers Destroy Horror*, *Nightmare Magazine*, and *Best Gay Stories*. When he's not creating Weird stories and inventing new monsters, Evan is a writing coach, film buff, tarot reader, pole dancer, and collector of malevolent plants. Everything you've heard about Florida is true.

Find out more at www.evanjpeterson.com.

BROKEN EYE BOOKS

Sign up for our newsletter at
www.brokeneyebooks.com

Welcome to Broken Eye Books! Our goal is to bring you the weird and funky that you just can't get anywhere else. We want to create books that blend genres and break expectations. We want stories with fascinating characters and forward-thinking ideas. We want to keep exploring and celebrating the joy of storytelling.

If you want to help us and all the authors and artists that are part of our projects, please leave a review for this book! Every single review will help this title get noticed by someone who might not have seen it otherwise.

And stay tuned because we've got more coming . . .

OUR BOOKS

The Hole Behind Midnight, by Clinton J. Boomer
Crooked, by Richard Pett
Scourge of the Realm, by Erik Scott de Bie
Izanami's Choice, by Adam Heine
Pretty Marys All in a Row, by Gwendolyn Kiste
The Great Faerie Strike, by Spencer Ellsworth
Catfish Lullaby, by A.C. Wise
Busted Synapses, by Erica L. Satifka
Boneset & Feathers, by Gwendolyn Kiste
Alphabet of Lightning, by Edward Morris
The Obsecration, by Matthew M. Bartlett
Better Living Through Alchemy, by Evan J. Peterson

COLLECTIONS
Royden Poole's Field Guide to the 25th Hour, by Clinton J. Boomer
Team Murderhobo: Assemble, by Clinton J. Boomer
Who Lost, I Found: Stories, by Eden Royce
Power to Yield and Other Stories, by Bogi Takács

ANTHOLOGIES
(edited by Scott Gable & C. Dombrowski)
By Faerie Light: Tales of the Fair Folk
Ghost in the Cogs: Steam-Powered Ghost Stories
Tomorrow's Cthulhu: Stories at the Dawn of Posthumanity
Ride the Star Wind: Cthulhu, Space Opera, and the Cosmic Weird
Welcome to Miskatonic University: Fantastically Weird Tales of Campus Life
It Came from Miskatonic University: Weirdly Fantastical Tales of Campus Life
Nowhereville: Weird Is Other People
Cooties Shot Required: There Are Things You Must Know
Whether Change: The Revolution Will Be Weird

Stay weird.
Read books.
Repeat.

brokeneyebooks.com
facebook.com/brokeneyebooks
instagram.com/brokeneyebooks

BROKEN
EYE
BOOKS

Printed in the USA
CPSIA information can be obtained
at www.ICGtesting.com
LVHW091107060824
787405LV00004B/128